PRAISE FOR

'Our new Book of the Week is *The Real Rebecca* by Anna Carey, a great new voice and definite Princess of Teen.'

Books for Keeps

'The story rattles along at a glorious rate – with plenty of witty asides. Rebecca herself is a thoroughly likeable heroine – angsty and mixed-up but warm-hearted and feisty.'

Books Ireland

Anna Carey is a freelance journalist from Drumcondra in Dublin who has written for the *Irish Times*, *Irish Independent* and many other publications. Anna joined her first band when she was fifteen and went on to sing and play with several bands over the next fifteen years. Her last band, El Diablo, released two albums and toured all over the country. *The Real Rebecca* was her first book, published in 2011, starring our heroine, and went on to win the Senior Children's Book prize at the Irish Book Awards. Readers haven't stopped asking for the next book.

Anna Carey

Irish Book Award Winner

THE O'BRIEN PRESS
DUBLIN

First published 2012 by The O'Brien Press Ltd,
12 Terenure Road East, Rathgar, Dublin 6, Ireland.
Tel: +353 1 4923333; Fax: +353 1 4922777
E-mail: books@obrien.ie
Website: www.obrien.ie
ISBN: 978-1-84717-344-7

A catalogue record for this title is available from the British Library.

1 2 3 4 5 6 7 8 9 10
12 13 14 15 16

Layout and design: The O'Brien Press Ltd.
Cover illustrations: Chris Judge
Printed and bound by CPI Group (UK) Ltd, Croydon, CR0 4YY

The paper used in this book is produced using pulp from managed forests.

The O'Brien Press receives assistance from

ACKNOWLEDGEMENTS

Many thanks to Brenda Boyne, Donna Sorensen, my patient and supportive editor Susan Houlden and everyone at the O'Brien Press; fellow giant-gas-jet winner Chris Judge for another wonderful cover; Helen Carr for general awesomeness and putting up with me borrowing her books for months; Miriam McCaul and Sam Murray for entertaining lunch outings when I was languishing in the creative doldrums; Fiona Cullen for the useful information on school musicals (much of which I then had to ignore for plot reasons); everyone on Twitter who encouraged, inspired and distracted me, especially Mary Macfarlane for helping me get a better handle on John's character and Sarah Franklin for general cheering; Sarra Manning and Sarah Webb for their much-appreciated support and encouragement; the late and much-missed Caroline Walsh for all her kindness; the extended Carey and Freyne families (especially the always-entertaining younger generation, Arlo, Cillian and Senan); Ju Ju, even though her noisiness distracted me when I was trying to write; and, as ever, my husband Patrick Freyne, for being funny and brilliant and coming up with the idea of Rebecca's parents having been in a musical themselves. And most of all, to everyone who read and enjoyed *The Real Rebecca*. I hope you like this book.

To my sisters Lisa, Jenny and Rachel.

Even though Jenny and Rachel actually got to be in school musicals and I didn't.

FRIDAY ☺

This is not what I thought Valentine's Day would be like this year.

For one, I didn't get a Valentine's card. Or even a Valentine's e-mail. Or even a Valentine's text. This wouldn't have been a big deal six months ago because, back then, I didn't know any boys who could send me any sort of Valentine's greetings. But for a while back in autumn, I was very optimistic about the future because quite a few good things had happened.

GOOD THINGS THAT HAPPENED LAST YEAR

1. I got a drum kit and started a band called Hey Dollface with my best friends.

2. We wrote some songs and played our first gig and even though I fell off the stage, people thought we were pretty good.

3. I met the coolest, nicest, most gorgeous boy ever,

who happened to deliver our newspapers every weekend, and he actually liked me and kissed me after the Battle of the Bands, despite the fact that I'd just fallen off a stage like an idiot, and then we started seeing each other.

So that was all brilliant. But then there were bad things too, including one thing so bad it almost cancels the good things out.

BAD THINGS THAT HAPPENED LAST YEAR

1. My mother wrote a *terrible* book about a stupid girl and everyone thought it was about me.
2. I got a mad new English teacher who was obsessed with my mother's books.
3. My hair continued to look like a sort of brown wavy mop.
4. My classmate Vanessa tried to force me to go

on a terrible reality programme about horrible spoiled teenagers and their mad birthday parties.

5. And my lovely perfect boyfriend (for three weeks) and his little brother and their stupid parents all moved to Canada.

Canada! I will never be happy again. When we got together after the Battle of the Bands, I thought we would live happily ever after. I was even too excited to write in this diary. But we only got to go out for a few weeks and then his dad got a job designing bridges or something in Vancouver, and off they went. And now it's February, and he's been gone for over two months, and I haven't been able to bring myself to write about it here until now. I will never love another boy again.

I said this to Alice a few weeks ago and she said, 'Are you sure? I mean, Bex, you're only fourteen. You're probably going to live for at least, like, five more decades. I think it might be quite difficult to avoid it. Loving another boy, I mean.'

Sometimes I think Alice does not have a very romantic soul. She doesn't understand my sorrow anymore. Today I mentioned my lack of Valentines and she just started talking about how this year's school musical is coming up, as if

I cared about our year putting on a production of *Mary Poppins* – Hey Dollface is the only musical outlet I need, thanks very much.

I didn't even bother telling her how disappointed I really was about the Valentine's card (or lack of it). To be honest, I felt a bit stupid hoping Paperboy would send me one. After he left, we chatted on Facebook and mailed each other all the time, but after a few weeks it all kind of … slowed down a bit. The last time I heard from him was last week (five days and thirteen hours ago) and he told me that his class were going skiing on a school trip. They're going to stay in a fancy ski lodge and have skiing and snowboarding lessons.

The most exciting school trip my class has ever been on was a geography trip to Glendalough, and that was only exciting because Ellie backed away while Miss Kelly was telling us about how the valley had been made by glaciers ploughing across the land, and because she wasn't looking where she was going, she fell into the lake (Ellie, of course, not Miss Kelly. Miss Kelly would never fall into a lake by accident. She is alert at all times, lest some environmental disaster take her by surprise). I mailed him back and told him about the lake incident but he hasn't replied yet. So much for romance.

I can't believe I was so happy a few months ago. After he kissed me outside the Battle of the Bands, I spent the entire week in a sort of daze. We hadn't even exchanged numbers or anything so I had to wait until he came for the paper money on Friday to see him again. I was a bit worried beforehand in case he turned up and told me he'd decided that the whole kissing thing had been a big mistake.

But he didn't. He still liked me. We stayed talking on my doorstep for ages until he realised he was really late for the rest of his paper round and had to run off to the next house on his list (but he kissed me very quickly when he said good-bye). And we went into town together the next day, and there was more kissing, and he was really funny and cool, and somehow even though I was nervous it was really easy to talk to him. I thought I'd be too intimidated by (a) his incredible gorgeousness and (b) the funny/cool aspect, but I wasn't. It turned out he lived in Clontarf (he cycled up to our estate to do his paper job) and of course he told me what his real name was and it is a very nice name (and not any of the names I guessed), but I don't want to write it down. I still think of him as Paperboy really, not least because Cass and

Alice refuse to call him anything else.

'He just looks like a Paperboy,' said Cass. 'It suits him.'

'Yes,' said Alice. 'I sort of think of Paperboy as being a real name these days.'

So do I, to be honest. If we'd got to go out for longer I might have got used to thinking of him as his actual name, but we didn't, so I didn't.

I think I must have been cursed at birth or something. I couldn't believe it when he told me about his dad's new job. His mum lost her job last year so there was no real reason (according to his parents) that they couldn't go straight away. It only took a few weeks for them to move (his cousin and her husband are renting his house from his parents so they didn't even have to sell anything) so it was all a bit of a blur. One minute he was there, the next he was in Canada. Surrounded by moose and mounties and Anne of Green Gables, as I said at the time. (Alice said that Canada wasn't like that at all, and that Vancouver was a much bigger, fancier city than Dublin, but for some reason I imagine him in a sort of rustic wilderness. Possibly riding a moose. And wearing some sort of checked shirt.)

Of course, as if to taunt me about how crappy my life has

become, my stupid big sister Rachel got a big card today from Saint Tom, her boyfriend who can do no wrong. It wasn't in the post this morning and I have to admit that when the post arrived and there was nothing but bills for Mum and Dad I was a bit glad because though Rachel has actually been surprisingly nice to me about the whole only-boy-I'll-ever-love-going-to-Canada thing, the fact that she has such a perfect boyfriend has been adding to my general misery. But of course the only reason Tom didn't send a card in the post was because he called around after school with the card and a big bouquet and took Rachel out for dinner in the posh little cheese place on Drumcondra Road. After they'd left, I said, 'I can't believe you're letting her go out for dinner on a school night. You know they're going to drink loads of wine there? Are you fine about that? Maybe you should go after them.'

Mum sighed.

'They won't have loads of wine,' she said. 'The staff know perfectly well they're underage. And it's only six o'clock – Rachel's going to be back by eight so she can do her homework then.'

The staff do know she's underage, it's true. We've been going there for a while with the whole family. So Rachel is unlikely to go on a massive wine-fuelled bender. Actually, I felt a bit mean trying to sabotage her romantic date. My broken romance has made me all bitter already. I feel a bit sad at the moment. I don't even feel like reading or watching TV or going online. I think I'll listen to some sad music and gaze out the window for a while.

LATER

I sat and stared out the window and listened to Nick Drake and thought about Paperboy for five minutes but had to give up and go downstairs because one of the little Mulligan kids who lives across the road was at her bedroom window too SPYING ON ME like the little freak she is. And when I looked up she started making sad faces and pretending to cry! She was mocking my anguish! Of course I turned around and tried to ignore her but after a while I couldn't help looking back, and when she saw me she started waving at me and doing a stupid dance. She had put on bright pink fluffy ear-muffs and kept gyrating around the place and shaking her bum at me and laughing. I tried to ignore it but even when my back was turned I just KNEW she was there wriggling around. So in the end I was driven out of my own bedroom. It's very difficult being properly miserable around here.

SATURDAY ☺

I can't believe my mother. She physically dragged me out of my bed this morning!

'I do not want you lying there all day moping,' she said. She had my duvet in her arms so there was no point in me trying to go back to bed again. 'I know you're still upset, but you can't act like you've given up on life! You're only fourteen!'

Why do people keep pointing out my age to me? It's not like I've forgotten how old I am.

'I'll be fifteen in a few months,' I said. 'And anyway, I haven't given up on life. I've just given up on getting any pleasure from it ever again. I am a hollow shell of a girl.'

My horrible mother sighed and rolled her eyes. She is *so* heartless. I can't believe she ever knew the anguish of love, like I do. Of course, she pretended she understood, but I know she doesn't. Otherwise she wouldn't shove me out of bed when I want to wallow in my misery.

'Rebecca, I can guarantee that you will enjoy life again,'

she said. 'Before I started going out with your dad I went to America for the summer and went out with a lovely American boy. When I went back to college I thought I'd be miserable forever. And that year I met your dad!'

Oh, like the prospect of meeting someone like my dad is going to cheer me up. I said this but Mum said if she hadn't met my dad, I would never have been born (which is true, obviously) and you never know what the future will hold.

In fact, she stood over me for ages spouting rubbish about how when you're my age 'every little thing feels like a tragedy' and how in a few years I'll look back at this time and wonder what I was so upset about. It was very annoying. Then she practically forced me to have a shower and get dressed because she was going to take me out. And what fun life-affirming activity did she have in store for me then? A trip to the cinema? Going into town to buy me a whole new wardrobe?

No! She dragged me out to the supermarket! Rachel and Dad were both out and she said she knew if I was home alone, I'd just 'sit there feeling sorry for myself' (I think it's a good thing I feel sorry for myself. God knows no one else does.)

So basically, I just spent my precious Saturday afternoon in Superquinn. I bet my mother didn't want to cheer me up, she just wanted a shopping slave. If she really wanted to show me how wonderful life is, surely there are better ways than making me wander around a supermarket with a wonky trolley looking at tins of beans? AND I had to carry loads of bags into the house afterwards and help unpack them! I feel even more sorry for myself than ever now, so her stupid plan didn't even work. Some mother she is.

LATER

My mother has 'rewarded' me for the trip to the supermarket by making one of my favourite dinners, lentil and chicken casserole. She didn't even make me rinse the lentils or chop up mushrooms for it (she made Rachel do it instead, which was the only bright spot in this stupid day). I would have liked to refuse it in protest at her uncaring treatment of me, but it smelled too delicious so I just ate it grudgingly instead. She didn't say anything else about trying to cheer me up. I hope she has realised that there's no point because I will never be cheerful again. I am going to stay up here in my room all evening listening to forlorn music. Luckily the Mulligans are out, so there's no chance of that kid tormenting me with her idiot dancing. I can ponder my misery in peace.

FIVE MINUTES LATER

The Mulligans must have come home because that stupid kid is at the window! And she's started dancing and making faces at me again! I'm going downstairs to get a hot drink. Hopefully she'll have got bored by the time I come back.

LATER

Went down to get that drink and found Mum and Rachel drinking hot chocolate and watching an old black and white musical in the sitting room. I didn't mean to stay, but the dancing was really cool so I found myself watching the rest of it with them. It turns out it is quite hard to feel miserable when you are watching people dance like that. I didn't tell Mum or Rachel that, though. I pretended I just happened to feel like sitting in that room for a bit. I don't think they would understand that just because you are VERY TEMPORARILY enjoying some old-fashioned dancing it doesn't mean that your heart is not broken forever.

SUNDAY ☼

Band practice this afternoon. We haven't been practising so much recently because Cass had a piano exam last week and her parents were making her practise Mozart etc all the time rather than the collected works of Hey Dollface. Which is a shame because without really realising it at the time, we actually have got better. And like many great artists over the years, my terrible personal tragedy has fuelled my creative powers.

'You know, on the plus side,' said Cass, about a week after Paperboy left, when I had more or less stopped crying all the time, 'not that there really is a plus side of course. But if there was, it would be that Paperboy going away will give you lots of material for songs.'

'It's true,' said Alice. 'I bet writing songs would be very therapeutic. So would banging those drums very hard, by the way.' We were sitting in our practice room out at Alice's place in Kinsealy at the time. Cass had come up with a new bassline and Alice was putting chords to it. I was meant to be drumming along, but I was so miserable I just tapped forlornly at the snare drum. After Alice said that, I started bashing them a bit harder and it did make me feel better. And so did writing some lyrics about what it's like to meet the boy of your dreams and then lose him to the wilds of Canada (or the Vancouver suburbs, if you're going to be finicky about it). The first one I wrote went like this:

Oh, oh, oh, oh, Canadian Boy
You've broken my heart by mistake
You went away when you were bringing me joy
If it's a nightmare I wish I could wake

I was quite proud of it, to be honest, though Cass pointed out (quite kindly) that Paperboy isn't actually Canadian. But 'boy from Clontarf who's gone to Canada' just looked weird, so Canadian Boy will have to do. We've turned it into quite a good song – we played it at practice today and it didn't sound bad. The thing about being a drummer, though, is that it's quite hard to write songs on your own. I mean, you can't work out chords or anything so it's hard to come up with a tune. Alice and Cass are both getting quite good at coming up with riffs and things on their own, and when we're all together I suggest different things to each of them, but because I can't play myself I have to rely on them to do everything.

The good thing is that I would really rather bash away at my drums than be a guitarist. And besides, Alice is getting really great at the guitar. I mean, she's had lessons so she was always able to do, like, the fancy classical stuff, but now she's really good at playing poppy choppy chords. And even though Cass used to act like she'd never be able to play her keyboard in an indie sort of way, she's a natural at coming up with basslines and cool noises. If we ever get a bass player, she'll be able to do even more. Even I've got better at the drums. It almost happened without my noticing it. I just kept bashing away and eventually I realised that I was able to play beats properly without actually thinking about it (of course, this means that as soon as I actually do think about what I'm doing, I instantly make a mistake. I think this shows that I am an instinctive natural musician).

But even my beloved drums can't cheer me up too much at the moment. The practice went pretty well today, and everything, but I still feel like a hollow shell of a girl. Since Paperboy left, I can't seem to feel enthusiastic about anything. And I'm starting to think Cass and Alice might be a bit bored with hearing about Paperboy, which, to be honest, I think is quite selfish of them. I know I'd be sympathetic if either of them met the love of her life and then he went off to the other side of the world after just three weeks. They don't know what it's like to suffer.

Cass even said today that the last lyrics I wrote (for a song with the working title 'The End of the World') were 'a bit too gloomy'. What does she know? She's having a great time! She's become great friends with Liz from Bad Monkey, the band we met at the Battle of the Bands, and they're off together practically every weekend.

In fact, I feel like I hardly see her any more. And Alice and I don't walk to school these days because a few months ago – just after the Battle of the Bands, actually – her mum got a new job and her route to work doesn't take her near my house now, so now she just drops Alice off near the school instead of near me. So I hardly see any of them. Well, apart from band practices. And actual school.

But still. I feel like our friendship needs a bit of a, I dunno, a kick or something. It's like I've forgotten how to talk to Cass and Alice about anything but how awful I feel. I know I want them to be sympathetic when I'm miserable, but I don't want them to HAVE to be sympathetic, if you know what I mean. I'm not sure even I know what I mean. I just wish I could get things back to the way they used to be, but it's like I've got stuck in a rut or something. And I want to get out of it. But how?

Still no mail from Paperboy, by the way.

LATER

I have decided to start expressing my woe in poetry. It's actually easier than writing song lyrics because it doesn't have to rhyme. Here is this evening's creation. I am quite proud of it.

Boy of paper
Paperboy
Across the sea
Why did you leave?
Apart from the fact that your dad
Got a job designing bridges?
My life
Now a shell

I think it is very poignant. And 'boy of paper' is quite clever if I say so myself. I think I should write more. I used to write quite a lot of stories when I was little, but I've sort of got out of the habit. Maybe my broken heart really will fuel my creative powers?

LATER

Can't think of anything to write now. Hmmm. I think I will go and watch some telly instead.

MONDAY ☼

I now have proof that my heart is broken – Miss Kelly's terrifying geography classes don't even bother me anymore. She spent today's class telling us that because of overpopulation the world won't be able to produce enough food to feed everyone, and so in a few years we will all have to eat insects and creepy crawlies in order to survive.

'They're an excellent source of protein,' she says. 'You get more protein per gram from a locust than from a chicken. I've tried them myself in Latin America.'

Everyone in the class was going 'Ugh!' and looking a bit unwell but of course that didn't stop Miss Kelly. The more scared we are, the more enthusiastic she gets. After about ten minutes of her raving about how delicious certain sorts of worms were, Jessie McCabe had to run out because she thought she was going to be sick. Normally I would feel the same. I used to have nightmares about tidal waves and water wars after her classes. But today I couldn't even bring myself to care. If I can't have Paperboy, I might as well just sit around eating insects.

At the end of the class I think Miss Kelly was a bit worried that she'd gone too far because she told us that not all insects were safe to eat and we shouldn't go out and try eating random bugs. Like any of us were sitting in the class going, 'Oh yes, Miss Kelly, eating grasshoppers in some sort of post-apocalyptic wasteland sounds brilliant, I think I'll start doing it straight away!' I mean, even though I might have lost all faith in the future and I don't care what happens, I'm not going to start eating bugs until I absolutely have to.

TUESDAY ☾

Cass and I went to the library after school. I love libraries; it's like going shopping for books only you're allowed to take away whatever you want for free! As long as you have space on your library card and don't owe loads of fines like SOME people (Cass). Unfortunately, when we went in to the library today, the first thing I saw was a display of new books with my mother's stupid teen novel right at the front with a 'Children's Book of the Month' sign on top of it. And next to it was a big coffee table book full of photos of Canada! Even the library has turned against me.

Anyway, I ignored this terrible display and headed for the teenage section, and we both found some good books (Well, they look good. Sometimes I just base my decisions on the cover). Cass took a deep breath and marched up to the desk to check hers out. When she scanned her ticket the librarian looked sternly at Cass and said, 'Ah, Miss McDermott. I hope you remember to bring these books back on time.' This is because Cass once took some books out and didn't give them back for about two years. The fines were enormous. She says once it reached a certain stage she was too embarrassed to give them back so she just didn't go to the library for a while. The library wrote to her house, but she hid the letters like some sort of criminal. To be honest, I'm surprised they ever let her have a library ticket again after all that, but clearly librarians are a forgiving lot. So once she had given back the books and paid a giant fine, they decided to let bygones be bygones. Well, most of them, anyway. This one hasn't forgotten. But she did give Cass the books.

In fact, I had a worse time checking books out because the librarian knows who I am too (we've all been going to this library since before we could read).

'Ah,' she said. 'I hope you saw your mother's book in our display! It's doing very well, you know. There's a waiting list for it and everything.'

She smiled at me like she thought I'd be pleased, whereas of course the thought of loads of people basically queuing up to read about that terrible Ruthie does not please me at all. Anyway, I just said, 'Oh, really?' in what I hope was a polite voice and luckily the librarian left it at that THANK GOD. I am fed up being polite to people about that stupid book, especially now that my life is even more of a tragedy.

On a more positive note, Cass thought of something when we were walking back from the library. She pointed out that if Miss Kelly is right about the future being electricity-free, then it's a good thing we like reading. At least we'll be able to amuse ourselves reading by candlelight when all the power has run out, and books will distract us from our insect-eating lives of toil. Cass is surprisingly practical sometimes.

I mentioned this to my mother when I got home and she said, 'I think your geography teacher is exaggerating a bit. I don't think we're going to be living without power or eating bugs any time soon.'

She would think that, though, because she and my dad are so hideously wasteful. They don't care about the environment at all. When I got home she was the only one there and yet the lights were on in practically every room in the house! If we do all end up huddling around a fire without any electricity in a few years, it'll be all her fault.

WEDNESDAY

Vanessa Finn's birthday party is on Saturday. And for some reason I am going to it. Even though, just a few months ago, I vowed (in front of lots of people, now I come to think of it, as well as in this diary) that there was no way I was ever going to her ridiculous extravaganza. I think I said I wouldn't even go if she paid me (which was a genuine possibility).

I can't believe we all gave in to Vanessa. A month or so ago we were all coming out of school and Cass and Alice were talking about how unfair Mrs O'Reilly had been in history class that morning, and I was thinking about Paperboy and wondering whether I could persuade my parents to move to Vancouver, when we realised that there was a camera crew outside the gates. And before any of us could get away, Vanessa appeared and started handing out giant sparkly invitations to everyone in the class and smiling at us like we were all best friends. We were all so stunned we just took them, and then Vanessa paraded off and got into a big posh car that was waiting nearby, as if this was how she always travels home from school (which is rubbish because she walks, normally).

As soon as she and her camera crew went off, everyone started talking about how mad she was and how there was no way any of us were going to her ridiculous party because she's always made it clear how awful it is for her having to slum it with us in a state school. She acts like we're all hardened criminals and she can't put her bag down for five seconds in case one of us nicks it (I have no idea why she thinks like this, by the way. She lives in a big house, but it's not, like, a castle. It's in Glasnevin surrounded by people who also go to state schools). Why would we want to go to a party for someone like that?

Also, none of us wanted to risk being caught on camera again by the 'My Big Birthday Bash' people, who would be filming it all for the reality show.

And then, a few days later, we were sitting in the cloakroom, drinking hot chocolate which Emma's big sister had kindly made for us with the sixth-year kettle, when Ellie said, 'You know, Vanessa's party could be kind of funny.'

'Funny peculiar, you mean,' said Cass.

'No, think about it,' said Ellie. 'I mean, it'll be completely mental. She's going to have a tank and a pony and God knows what else. It might be ... you know, fun.'

'Ellie,' I said. 'This is Vanessa. Remember when my mum's book came out and she pretended to be friends with me in a really creepy way because she thought it would impress the 'My Big Birthday Bash' people? She's crazed. And then she wanted me and Cass and Alice to play at her party and had a tantrum when I fell off the stage because she thought it had spoiled her chances of getting on that awful show.'

'She is pretty crazed,' agreed Cass.

'I know,' said Ellie, 'but that's what could make the party funny. I mean, don't you want to see what she looks like riding around in a tank? It'll be hilarious!'

'Hmmm,' said Cass. 'Good point.'

'But if we all turn up it'll only encourage her!' I said. 'She'll think it's okay to carry on like that!'

'To be honest, I don't think she'll even notice,' said Ellie. 'I mean, she thinks it's okay anyway. I bet even if only three people turn up, it wouldn't make any difference to her.'

'She's pretty good at ignoring reality,' said Cass. 'Remember when you kept trying to tell her you weren't going to her party and she just acted like you were agreeing with her? And let's not forget that she's still convinced that all of us are from the slums because our parents are teachers and guards and stuff, instead of, I dunno, royalty.'

'True,' I said.

'But isn't it a bit mean?' said Alice. 'I mean, we don't like Vanessa.'

'We certainly don't,' I said.

'Well, if you heard of people going to the party of someone they didn't like just to laugh at it, you'd think that was mean, wouldn't you?'

We all paused. When you put it like that, it did sound pretty horrendous. Except ...

'The thing is,' said Cass, 'there's a big difference between going to laugh at the party of someone who's invited you because she, y'know, actually likes you and wants you to be there, and someone who's inviting absolutely everyone and doesn't care about any of them and has also, let's not forget, shouted at some of them in public.'

'Hmm,' said Alice. 'I suppose. But still ...'

Sometimes Alice is just too good. She's definitely gooder than me. So anyway, we all thought about it and gradually, over the next week or so, it turned out that we all sort of wanted to go. Even though it's being filmed. We figured we can manage to avoid the cameras. It's worth going just, as Cass said one night when we talked on the phone, 'to see the tank. And the pink pony. If that's still happening. I always thought that sounded a bit too ridiculous, even for Vanessa.'

'I wouldn't put it past her,' I said. 'She said she was going to get it dyed specially.'

'But where?' said Cass. 'I mean, who can you ask to dye a pony pink? A vet? I can't imagine a decent vet would do it. Imagine if you took Bumpers down to the vet and asked them to dye him pink.'

'It'll be hard enough getting the vet to give Bumpers his booster shots after the last time,' I said. 'She said she'd never met such a loud cat. But maybe ponies are different. They're not as wriggly and bitey.'

'Well, there's only one way to find out,' said Cass cheerfully. 'Come on! It'll distract you from mooning around moping over Paperboy.'

'I don't moon!' I cried. 'And I definitely don't mope.'

'Okay, okay,' said Cass, but I don't think she was telling the truth. I think she really thinks I've been mooning and moping.

Anyway, that moping and mooning conversation was about two weeks ago. A few days later, we all e-mailed our RSVPs to Vanessa, which was when we started realising that deciding to go her party may not have been a good idea after all because she spent the next fortnight parading around the school boasting about how brilliant the stupid thing was going to be and how she had to hurry home after school every day (like anyone cared) to meet the film crew and show them her stage set and her outfits. She's being even more obnoxious and rude than usual. And then we all got sent back forms for our parents to sign, saying it was okay for us to appear on 'My Big Birthday Bash', and promising that we wouldn't put anything about the party online before the stupid programme aired. It was ridiculous.

But despite all this, I know that on Saturday we're all going to be waiting outside the school for the bus Vanessa's parents have hired to take us to some castle in the middle of nowhere that they've rented for the party.

Mum says this is 'morbid curiosity' and that we are all just going because we think it's going to be a big disaster. She may have a point. Oh well, maybe Cass is right and it will take my mind off Paperboy and stop me wondering why he didn't even send me a Valentine text. And I have to admit, I do kind of want to see the tank.

He still hasn't mailed or messaged me.

THURSDAY

I am the worst friend ever!

I am wracked with guilt. I had a big ... well, not quite a fight, but definitely a 'scene' with Alice today. And Alice doesn't really do fights. Or get really angry. But she was properly angry today. And it was my fault. And I feel really bad.

It all happened just after school. Cass was off sick today (she texted me this morning to say the entire family had got food poisoning. They went out to dinner yesterday as a special treat for her dad's birthday and they all ended up puking all night. Which must have been pretty disgusting because there's four of them and only one loo) and so it was just me waiting with Alice at the gate for her dad to turn up and collect her. And we were sort of talking about the old days when we used to walk together and then I said, 'Hey, guess who I saw today on my way in? Bike Boy! Remember him?'

Bike Boy's real name is Richard and he is a boy who has always cycled past us on our way to school and then turned up with his band at the Battle of the Bands. Alice used to fancy him a bit and then got talking to him at the Battle. But about a week later she stopped walking to school so she didn't really get to see him again (I think we saw him in the distance cycling ahead of us down Calderwood Road one day, but that was it and then she started getting a lift straight to school). I still see him every so often and sometimes we nod at each other in greeting, but I don't really notice him or indeed any other boys because my heart belongs to Paperboy and always will.

So anyway, when I said, 'Remember him?' Alice looked a bit funny and said, 'Of course I remember him.'

And I said, 'Oh. I wasn't sure if you did because you haven't really mentioned him in months and months. So I didn't know if you've really thought about him much since the whole Battle of the Bands thing.'

There was a bit of a pause and then Alice said, 'Oh my God, of course I have.'

I just stared at her and said, 'What? Really?' in a surprised sort of way.

And Alice looked really annoyed and said, 'I've been thinking about him ever since the Battle of the Bands. I thought something might happen, but then I stopped walking to school with you so I didn't see him. And I've been really, really sad about it, but I haven't said one word to you about it because I knew it wasn't a big deal in comparison with your wonderful new romance with Paperboy and then him going off to Canada, so I didn't feel like I had a right to be so upset. But you never even asked whether I was upset or not! You never even thought about it!'

I felt absolutely awful. Usually when I am given out to I get all annoyed because I don't think the other person is being fair, but the horrible thing about this was that Alice was right. I hadn't thought about her and Bike Boy. I'd been totally caught up in my own stuff. I was going to say something, but Alice was on a roll of anger (this was all very unusual for her).

'And I'd tell myself that obviously your situation was much worse, and you had actually gone out with Paperboy and I'd only had about two conversations with Bike Boy and barely knew him, but, still, I felt really bad, and you knew I liked him and then you forgot all about it!' she cried. 'Because you're just thinking about yourself and how miserable you are all the time! Me and Cass could ... could be, I dunno, run over by a bus and you probably wouldn't notice!'

'I would!' I said, which I suppose was a bit of stupid thing to say.

'Would you?' said Alice, in the same cross, kind of sarky voice, which wasn't like her at all. She was getting very red in the face. 'You know, Cass still sometimes asks whether I'm okay about him. And she tells me whenever she sees him around the area. She didn't forget all about other people's problems!'

And I started to get angry and say 'I didn't forget about your problems!' but I stopped after 'I' because of course, I totally had. So instead I said, 'I'm really sorry Alice. Really, really sorry.'

'Good,' said Alice, and burst into tears. And then of course, being Alice, she started apologising herself, and I kept saying 'It's me who should be apologising' (though I was secretly relieved she wasn't still yelling at me, even though I deserved it. I really am a terrible person). So in the end we both apologised, and I gave her a hug, and I kept saying I was sorry until her dad turned up, and she sent me a text about five minutes ago saying she was sorry for yelling at me, not that she really did yell, so there has been a lot of apologising and I think we are still friends. Unless she is just being nice to me in a polite, Alice-ish way and is secretly full of hatred and rage. But I don't think so.

I feel really bad, though. A part of me is thinking 'Well, my problems are properly serious, and she barely knew Bike Boy!' But then I remember how absolutely awful I felt that day when I saw Paperboy in town with a girl and thought she was his girlfriend. I felt like my heart was broken even though I'd only talked to him once or twice. So poor Alice was probably feeling that bad, and I didn't even think of her woe. I know I was worried that we were all growing apart, but this is even worse than I imagined. And she and Cass are talking about Alice's angst together without me. But what I can I do?

LATER

Okay. I will start by making up some new rules for myself. And I will stick to them.

REBECCA RAFFERTY'S RULES FOR LIVING

1. I will not go on about Paperboy all the time and tell my friends that I am now just a hollow shell of a girl (even though I am).

2. I will not mope. At least, when I am with other people.

3. I will find ways to do more interesting stuff with Cass and Alice, so we can bond and stuff and things will get back to normal.

4. I will ask my friends about their problems more often.

Still no mail from Paperboy. I wish I didn't get my hopes up every time I check the computer. But I do.

FRIDAY ☺

I'm writing this in history, where Mrs O'Reilly is telling us about the Renaissance, or something to do with the olden days. I'm not really listening, which I suppose is kind of obvious as I'm writing here. I'm sitting next to Caroline, aka Vanessa Finn's sidekick, so I can't even draw amusing pictures of Cass dressed as historical figures and taunt her with them, which is what I usually do when I'm bored in history. Mrs O'Reilly decided that Cass and I can't sit next to each other anymore. Cass got caught drawing a picture of Mrs O'Reilly dressed as Queen Elizabeth I and giving out to two girls who looked a bit like me and Cass. But we both got into trouble for it, which is extremely unfair if you ask me, not that Mrs O'Reilly did. She said that I was clearly egging Cass on and I shouldn't think she hadn't noticed that I seemed to spend a lot of history classes showing Cass something in my copybook. She must have eyes in the back of her head. I never show Cass my amazing portraits unless O'Reilly is writing on the board.

Anyway, I still feel very guilty about the whole Alice and Bike Boy thing. I think she has sort of forgiven me, but I still feel bad. I told her and Cass about my new rules (apart from the bonding one in case they thought I was weird) and they were quite impressed, though Alice seemed a bit worried about it.

'I'm not annoyed with you anymore, you know,' she said. 'I don't want you to think you've got to, like, reform for my sake.'

But I told her that I still wanted to change my ways. To try and make up for my dreadful-friendness I told her that I will steal Rachel's nicest Chanel lipstick tomorrow, the one Alice always says she wishes she could afford, so she can wear it to Vanessa's mad party (I often put it on at home before going out when Rachel's not around, but I've never dared take it out of the house before). I don't think it will make up for not even noticing that her heart was broken, but at least it's a start.

And I am sticking to my new rule and I am not going on about Paperboy. I haven't even mentioned the fact that I haven't heard from him in ages. I hate checking my mail or Facebook now because my stomach gets all churned up. And then when I realise there's nothing my tummy feels like it's sunk into the floor. He never really posts updates on Facebook so I can't even find out what he's doing. I almost wish he'd just mail me and tell me he never wants to hear from me again; it would be better than just waiting all the time. Except I don't really wish that. I really just wish he'd come home and go out with me again.

But I haven't mentioned any of this to Cass and Alice, or the fact that now he has gone forever Fridays are nothing more than a torment. Smyth's the newsagent got a new paperboy who is not attractive at all and whenever he rings I am reminded of my tragic state. Every time I go out to give him his money it is like a dagger in my heart. A dagger made of fivers and the *Irish Times*. No, that doesn't sound quite right. But anyway, it makes me all sad and reminds me of the days when I got all excited every time the door bell rang on a Friday. It seems like a million years ago now.

Oh well, at least Vanessa's party is tomorrow. I can't believe I'm kind of looking forward to it. It shows what a sorry state my life is in when the only thing I have to look forward to is a crazy person's ridiculous birthday party.

SATURDAY ☺

Well, I was right about the party distracting me from my Paperboy-related misery. It was so completely ridiculous that it has blocked all other thoughts from my head. I think I'd better write about it straight away because if I don't I'll start thinking I imagined the whole thing. I really don't know why we went now. Even my own family couldn't believe I was going. When I was getting ready, my mum came in.

'Okay, forgive me if I've missed something here,' she said. 'But don't you hate Vanessa or whatever her name is?'

'Well,' I said, putting on my best strappy shoes. 'Sort of. A bit.'

'So why exactly are you going to her party then?' said Mum. 'And don't say because it'll be terrible and you want to see how bad it is, because that's not really a good thing.'

'But it will! It'll be funny,' I said. 'I mean, it'll be so ridiculous, and she's so awful ...'

'So essentially, Rebecca, you're going to the party of a girl you don't like just to laugh at it?' said Mum. 'That isn't very nice.' She sounded a bit like Alice, which was quite worrying.

'Mum, it's Vanessa!' I said. 'She doesn't like any of us

either, and she invited us anyway! She just wants people to cheer for her.'

'Hmmm,' said Mum in a disapproving sort of way. So much for her trying to cheer me up. She doesn't seem bothered about my traumas now. My dad's even worse, though. He's forgotten all about them. The other day he asked me, totally cheerfully, if I'd heard from 'that nice kid who used to collect the paper money' recently. He hadn't even noticed my anguish! My parents are as bad as each other. Sometimes I think they just don't care about me at all.

In the end Mum gave me a lift down to the school gates this afternoon, where we'd been told to wait for the bus that was taking us to Vanessa's 'Big Birthday Bash'. She wanted to get out of the car and wait until the bus turned up, but luckily I managed to persuade her not to. I have seen my mother try to be cool and chat with a gang of girls my age, and it is hideously embarrassing.

So anyway, she drove off THANK GOD and there we all were standing at the side of the road. As Alice said, as we shivered in our party frocks, 'I'm not really sure how this happened.'

I looked around at the rest of our class, all of whom looked equally bemused. 'Neither am I,' I said.

'I think Vanessa's hypnotised us all,' said Cass gloomily. 'I have no idea why I'm here.'

All our reasons for going didn't seem very important when we were standing there with bare legs in the freezing cold.

'I think this might be a bit of a disaster,' said Alice. And as it turned out, it kind of was, especially for poor old Alice, as you will see.

But, actually, the bus journey itself was quite fun. The entire class was there (even sneery Karen Rodgers, who has been a bit subdued since her sidekick/minion Alison told her to shut up at the Battle of the Bands last year) so it was a bit like being on a school tour (though not an impressive one like Paperboy's ski lodge adventure). And Vanessa (or rather, the people from the telly programme – there's no way Vanessa went to any trouble herself) had decorated the bus with balloons and a big banner that said 'Vanessa's Big Birthday Bash!'

Soon everyone, even Karen, was singing along to Jessie's iPod, which we'd plugged into the bus's sound system. Some of the music was kind of cheesy but it didn't matter. We were all just messing around. It was actually like a mini-party – most of us had brought drinks (no booze, of course, though as

Cass said later, if anything could make us turn to drink, it'd be Vanessa) and bags of crisps and stuff. Emma produced a giant bag of Percy Pigs and I ate so many I started to feel a bit funny.

Jessie is going to audition for the school musical and she did some very funny actions to all the songs. Ellie joined in, although she doesn't want to perform in the musical; she wants to work on the costumes. She is quite dramatic herself, though. Perhaps this is because her mother is very melodramatic as well as hippy-ish (let us never forget that Ellie's real name is Galadriel after the elf queen from the *Lord of the Rings*), so Ellie has spent her entire life living with someone who is always sweeping out of rooms in flowing cloaks and things. Seriously. Her mum has a cloak. I've seen it. It's made out of velvet and has stars embroidered all over it.

So anyway, it was all good fun. And I had managed to swipe Rachel's lipstick (she will KILL me if she discovers I've taken it, especially as she hasn't figured out yet that I've discovered where she hides her make-up bag. She keeps putting it in different places so I can't get at it. She is a very suspicious person). Alice put on the lipstick when we were on a smooth bit of road (she didn't dare try it until we got on the motorway in case the bus zoomed around a corner and she got lipstick all over her face) and it looked lovely. It is a magical colour that suits everyone. I gave a few more people a go as well, just to be nice. I'm sure Rachel wouldn't mind. It was all lots of fun, anyway.

'You know, maybe we can just stay and have our own party on this bus,' said Cass. 'I bet we'd have a better time.'

She was probably right. But after a while, we were out in the countryside, and the bus turned into a giant set of gates and drove up a very long drive to an absolutely ginormous house. Well, a castle really – it turns out it was called Ashford Towers and it's mostly used for very posh weddings.

The bus pulled up at the very impressive entrance and we all got out and stared at the castle wondering what on earth we'd got ourselves into. Then a tall, skinny, very stressed-looking woman in a tight black dress and a phone headset thing came out of the gigantic front door along with another camera crew. They all looked miserable. I was just thinking that the stressed woman seemed strangely familiar when Alice said, 'Wasn't she the TV woman who was with Vanessa at the Battle of the Bands?' And she was. She looked a bit older though, which isn't really surprising when you remember that she's been spending a lot of time with Vanessa recently. That would age anyone by about fifty years.

'Oh, you're all here,' she said. 'Great. I was beginning to get a bit worried.' We all started moving towards the door but she said, 'Wait!' and we all froze. 'You can't go in yet. Vanessa will be arriving soon and we want everyone outside when she gets here. Stay there and I'll get the others.'

'Others?' said Ellie. 'I didn't think Vanessa actually had any friends, apart from Caroline, of course.'

'Maybe she's paid people to pretend,' said Cass.

And when a bunch of girls and boys came out of the house and paraded down the steps, I thought Cass might be right. The girls were all orange and wearing loads of make-up and had perfectly straight glossy hair and tiny little party dresses and really high heels. And the boys were all orange too, although their hair was gelled.

'Who on earth are they?' said Alice.

'Right,' said the woman in the black dress whose name, I remembered, was Sarah. 'Okay, Vanessa's class from St Dominic's, can you line up on either side of the drive? And the kids from ... is it the music class?'

'Music, dance, and theatre,' said one girl, tossing her shiny, shiny hair.

We all looked at each other in surprise. How did we not know Vanessa went to a music class? And dance and theatre too, of course. Surely if she was in a class like that she'd have been boasting about it constantly.

'Yes,' said Sarah. 'Okay, you lot come up the front, near the steps. Yes, that's perfect. Hang on a sec ...' She paused and then spoke into the headset. 'Yeah, they're all ready.' She turned back to us. 'Right, everyone, Vanessa is on her way.'

The camera crew bustled around, getting into their places. Then, in the distance, we heard a rumbling sound. Someone shouted 'Action'. And this giant pink tank came rumbling up the drive, with someone with absolutely huge hair peering out the top. It was Vanessa. As the tank got nearer, she stuck more of herself out of the hole and started waving regally at us. She was wearing a sparkly gold and pink dress with a ginormous frilly flower at the neck.

'Oh. My. God,' said Cass.

We all stood and stared in silence as the tank came up to the steps, where the shiny orange people were jumping around and cheering. Then, over the cheering, we heard a familiar shriek.

'No, no, NOOO!'

It was Vanessa. 'They didn't cheer!' she screeched. 'They're all meant to be cheering and they didn't! Just the ones at the steps were cheering!'

'Okay, okay,' said Sarah in a soothing sort of voice, like she was talking to a maniac who had to be kept calm in case she went on a killing spree. Which I suppose she was. 'We'll do it again. Okay, everyone from St Dominic's, this time I want you to all cheer and jump up and down when Vanessa comes down. Okay?'

We all just stared at her. A few people mumbled, 'Okay ...'

'Right,' said Sarah. 'Let's get the tank back to the bottom of the drive and reshoot.'

The tank rumbled off. Cass, Alice and I stared at each other.

'I'm not cheering for that goon,' said Cass.

'What do you think will happen if we don't?' I asked. 'Maybe Vanessa will turn the tank on us. I wouldn't put it past her.'

'I don't care,' said Alice, bravely. 'One of my great-granddads was shot for standing up to the Nazis! If he can do that, we can stand up to Vanessa.'

'Well, when you put it like that ...' I said.

'Alice,' said Cass, 'I don't think you can really compare

standing up to Vanessa to standing up to Hitler.'

'I know,' said Alice. 'That's my point. If he was brave enough to stand up to fascism, we can do this little thing. Who's with me?'

It was very inspiring, to be honest. I crossed my arms and clamped my mouth shut so it would be very obvious that I wasn't cheering.

'But maybe,' said Ellie, who was next to us, 'if we don't cheer they'll keep making us do it again and again until we give in. And I'm freezing. To be perfectly honest, I will do anything to get indoors.'

'Oh,' said Cass.

Ellie was right, it was very cold. The tank was coming back up the drive again, and as it approached Jessie and Ellie and Emma started going 'Whoo hoo!' in a sort of sarcastic way. Alice kept her mouth shut and folded her arms. Cass and I decided to compromise and clapped very, very slowly. I hope Alice's great-granddad wasn't looking down on us from heaven in disgust at our cowardice.

Luckily, enough people were cheering to please Princess Vanessa, and when she got to the steps she waved and cried, 'Hi, everyone! Great to see you all!' as if she hadn't just seen us all two minutes earlier when she'd been screaming at us like a psychopath. A sparkly pink ladder was produced and Vanessa got out of the tank and climbed down it. Her dress was very tiny and glittery, and she was wearing gold shoes with red soles. She went up the steps and all the glossy music and theatre people started squealing and jumping around and hugging her.

'Hey, where's Caroline?' said Cass, which was a good question. We thought Caroline was Vanessa's best friend, but now she was nowhere to be seen.

'Wait,' said Emma. 'There she is, look! Behind that orange girl in the black dress.'

Caroline was at the back of the crowd of music and theatre people. She was just standing there while Vanessa hugged and squealed at the others.

We all felt a bit sorry for her, to be honest. Her devotion to Vanessa is annoying, but the least she deserved was to be, like, acknowledged at Vanessa's stupid party. She was wearing a very nice dress, but she looked a bit uncomfortable. She certainly wasn't shrieking as much as the others. Suddenly Vanessa grabbed her and gave her a giant hug. From a distance, it was hard to tell whether it was a real hug or whether she was just doing it for the camera. I'd like to think Vanessa appreciates Caroline, even though both of them are pretty irritating.

Then Sarah appeared and told us all to go into the main hall. Vanessa and her mysterious new friends led the way and strutted into the building as the rest of us followed behind (not strutting).

The hall was a big room panelled in wood with a small stage at one end between two sweeping flights of stairs. There were giant pink bean bags in the corners.

'This is actually not as fancy as I expected,' said Cass. 'I thought there'd be, like, a throne, or something.'

Then, suddenly, Vanessa was up on the stage with a microphone in her hand. It wasn't an ordinary microphone, though, like the ones we use at gigs. It was bright pink and sparkly and it wasn't attached to a lead and an amplifier.

'Hi, everyone!' Her voice boomed from the speakers on each side of the stage thing. 'Thank you SO much for coming! It means so much to me!'

'It means so much to me to be on telly, more like,' muttered Cass. 'Like she cares whether any of us came or not. We're just here to yell and make the room look full.'

'Ssssh,' said Ellie. 'If we talk over her, she'll have another tantrum and do it again and we'll be here all day.'

'Good point,' said Cass.

'At least we're indoors,' said Emma. 'And warm. Which is better than ten minutes ago.'

Then we all shut up because Vanessa had obviously noticed that people were talking. She looked like she could be on the verge of another fit of rage, and none of us wanted that.

'I just want to say,' she said, 'that you're all very welcome to my big … birthday … bash!'

And then we all did shriek because about a million shiny pink balloons suddenly fell down on top of our heads. None of us had looked up at the ceiling when we came in because we were so busy wondering about Vanessa and her mysterious new friends, so we hadn't noticed the balloons up there.

'There is a LOT of pink at this party already,' said Cass, fighting her way through some balloons.

'And we haven't even got to the pony yet,' I said.

'That pony had better turn up,' said Cass, 'or I'm going to be very disappointed.'

Terrible cheesy music started to play, and all Vanessa's new friends started whooping and dancing around. I looked at Cass and Alice.

'This is going to be a very long day,' said Alice.

'Ooh, look!' said Ellie. 'Food! And drinks!'

Waiters in pink uniforms were moving through the crowd, carrying trays. Some were filled with glasses of fizzy drinks, others with lots of delicious-looking canapé things. We grabbed some Cokes and – yes! Mini-burgers! – and watched the crowd. Some girls from our class were dancing, but most were just standing around wondering what to do. All the cameras were on Vanessa's new chums, though. They were laughing and throwing their hair around and high-fiving each other.

'They don't look real,' said Alice. 'I mean, they're like characters from *Laurel Canyon* or something.'

'They can't live in our neck of the woods,' I said. 'We'd have noticed them by now.'

'Yeah, because one of them would have hit us in the face with her ginormous shiny mane,' said Cass. 'They're flicking their hair around so much they'll put someone's eye out.'

'In fairness,' said Emma, chomping on a mini-burger, 'the food is pretty good.'

Emma was right. We sat in a corner on one of the giant pink beanbags and stuffed our faces and talked. It was quite fun for a while.

'You know, even though the music's pretty awful,' I said, 'this isn't so bad. I mean, there's mini-burgers, and bean-bags ...'

'And dancing goons,' said Cass, pointing at the glossy gang, who were pouting at the cameras. 'Speaking of goons, where's Vanessa?'

She was nowhere to be seen. Poor Caroline was dancing slightly awkwardly next to all the hair-flickers, but there was no sign of her ruler. Then the music stopped.

'Ooh, maybe the pony's coming!' said Cass. There was a trumpeting sound, and the two big doors at the end of the hall opened (some more cameras were already directed in that direction). Loads of smoky dry ice floated out the doorway, lit by pink spotlights. I have to admit, I did hope the pony was about to appear.

Then a booming voice cried, 'All hail Princess Vanessa!' And suddenly Vanessa appeared in the doorway. She had changed into a long flowing sparkly dress like something Alice's Barbie had when we were little (I never had a Barbie because my mother didn't believe in them. She thought Barbie was a bad role model for little girls. And after seeing Vanessa today, I had to admit for the first time that she might have had a point). As if the Barbie dress wasn't mad enough, she was also wearing a crown.

'Oh my GOD,' said Cass. 'Are we expected to, I dunno, bow down and worship her now?'

'I certainly hope not,' I said.

'Well, I'm not doing it even if we are,' said Alice. 'I'd rather die.'

'I don't think you're going to have to choose between death and worshipping Vanessa,' I said. Although really, if Vanessa had her own way, I'm pretty sure she'd love to shoot anyone who didn't do whatever she wanted.

Vanessa was waving regally to the crowd, most of whom were just gawping at her. The dancing goons, of course, were cheering and whooping and jumping up and down. I bet they have no voices left tomorrow.

'Come!' cried Vanessa. 'Come and join the revels at my fairytale ball!' And she turned around and swept into the next room, her flowing skirt fluttering after her.

'Her WHAT?' said Cass.

'Has she actually gone mad?' said Emma. 'I think she has. This is great.'

We all followed the rest of the guests into the next room.

And I have to admit, I was impressed. It was a giant old-fashioned ballroom, with big old gold-framed mirrors on the walls, and there were little twinkling lights everywhere. The lights were all pink and purple and people were throwing glitter down from a sort of balcony thing high up above the entrance so the light was all sparkly. There was a band at one end of the room playing swirly classical music.

'Wow,' said Alice.

'Okay,' said Cass. 'This is kind of cool. Ooh, look, I think there's actually a throne over there!'

Then Vanessa popped up on yet another podium/stage thing with a microphone on it (there seemed to be one in every room) and said, 'Let the fairytale princes sweep you away!' And then, as romantic music started to play, we realised there were all these strange boys in posh suits standing around the room. They started coming up to people and asking them to dance. As the cameras rolled, one of the fairytale princes whispered something in Karen Rodgers's ear, and a moment later she was whirling around the dance floor.

'Oh my God,' said Alice. 'Has she ... hired people to dance with our class?'

'I hope none of them come near us,' I said.

'This is like when you go to a pantomime and someone comes off the stage into the audience and tries to get people to join in,' said Cass. 'In other words, my worst nightmare. Can we hide somewhere?'

Luckily, in all the dry ice and pink sparkly glitter, it was easy for me, Cass, Alice, Jessie, Ellie and Emma to sneak back into the hall. Everyone else was in the ballroom so it was nice and peaceful out there. We kicked our way through the balloons and over to a pile of beanbags. But when we reached the bags there, to our surprise, was a girl we'd never seen before. She was lying on a beanbag eating a mini-burger.

'Oh, hello,' she said, sitting up.

'Um, hello,' said Alice. 'Why aren't you in the ballroom?'

'I think I've done my duty for one day,' said the girl.

'What do you mean?' said Ellie.

The girl looked at us. 'Are you good friends of Vanessa?'

None of us said anything. We didn't want to tell the truth, in case this girl was one of Vanessa's best mates or her cousin, or something.

'I'll take that as a no,' said the girl. She had a round, friendly face and glossy black hair with a very nice sleek fringe, the sort of fringe I wish I could have but never can because of my stupid weird half-wavy hair. 'Well, I'm not a friend of Vanessa either. I'm in her dancing and theatre class. Or at least, the class she joined a month ago. She came along to learn how to do a special dance for this crazy party, and she got a bunch of people from the class to come along to the party to dance around in front of the cameras.'

We all stared at each other. So that's where the shiny orange people had come from.

'So why aren't you, well, dancing around in front of the cameras?' asked Alice.

'Hmmm,' said the girl. 'It's not really my sort of thing. I mean, I like dancing, obviously, otherwise I wouldn't be in the class, but not … well, not dancing at a mad stranger's party, pretending I'm her best mate. No offence,' she added quickly, 'if you are her best mates.'

'We're not,' said Cass firmly. 'I'm Cass, by the way.'

'I'm Jane,' said the girl.

'So none of those dancing people are Vanessa's friends?' I asked.

'I doubt it,' said Jane. 'She's only been going to the class for about a month. She said she wanted all of us to come to her party cos she wanted there to be – these are her words, not mine

– at least a few people who looked good in front of the camera.'

We all stared at each other.

'Well!' said Alice.

'Just when you thought she couldn't get any worse,' said Cass.

'If it's any consolation, I don't think she was including me in that group,' said Jane. 'I just don't think she had the nerve to tell me to go away. Although,' she added, 'I think she might have wanted me in there as the token Asian girl. You know, to make everything look glamorous and multicultural and stuff.'

'That does sound like the sort of thing Vanessa would do,' agreed Cass.

'I should probably warn you, she's got us all to do something really terrible later,' said Jane. 'I can't tell you, though, because it's top secret and if it got out that anyone knew, she'd probably have me shot.'

'I knew it,' said Alice.

Even though we were all horrified by Vanessa's awfulness, it was kind of fun sitting out there. The whole thing was so weird and unlike our normal daily life that I had totally forgotten to think about Paperboy. It was like the olden days before my heart was broken and I became a miserable shell of a girl. We were all just laughing and messing about. Maybe if we had a crazy big party every day – or even every week – I'd feel like me and Cass and Alice were properly close again.

Jane was really cool. It turns out that she's from Glasnevin, like Vanessa, and she's known Vanessa since she was tiny (the rest of us have only had to put up with Vanessa for the last year and almost-a-half, but poor Jane has had fourteen years of her). Vanessa's mum and Jane's mum are friends, which is how Mrs Finn found out about the dancing and theatre and whatever-it-is class.

'I started going there in September,' said Jane. 'But I think I'll give it up after this term and find another class. It's awful. It's not like I thought it would be. Everyone's like Vanessa – well, maybe not as mad. But they're all very ... showbizzy. I mean, you've seen what they're like.'

We all thought of the squealing, glossy gang in the next room, tossing their shiny shiny hair all over the place. Cass shuddered.

'So why did you join the class in the first place?' asked Ellie.

Jane sighed. 'Well, I like dancing. I used to go to ballet when I was little. And I like acting,' she said. 'But ... I dunno. The class isn't fun. Everyone's just obsessed with being famous.'

'Like Vanessa,' I said. 'Once she decided to apply to be on 'My Big Birthday Bash' she got even worse than she used to be.'

'Especially worse to you,' said Emma. And she told Jane how Vanessa had decided I was almost a celebrity because my mum wrote that book, and how Vanessa and tried to use me to get on 'My Big Birthday Bash'.

'And then we played at the Battle of the Bands and Bex fell off her drum stool and we didn't win, so Vanessa decided we'd done it on purpose and had a huge mental tantrum in front of the producers and everyone,' said Cass. 'But they loved it and that's why they chose her to be on the show. The more deranged the better, apparently.'

'Wow,' said Jane. 'I remember Mrs Finn telling my mum that Vanessa had taken them to some sort of concert and the producers had been really impressed, but she didn't mention why ...'

'What are her parents like, anyway?' asked Ellie. 'We've never actually seen them. Are they as mad as her? I mean, how did she turn out like this?'

But before Jane could answer, the door to the main ballroom opened and Sarah, the 'Big Birthday Bash' producer, slipped out and closed it behind her. Then she saw us lolling around on the beanbags and strode over to us. She didn't look happy.

'Girls!' she said. 'What are you doing out here? Everyone's meant to be in there dancing with the fairytale princes.' She looked more closely at me, Cass and Alice. 'Aren't you the girls who were in that band?'

'Um, yes,' said Alice.

'Ah,' said Sarah. 'I don't suppose you'd like to get on stage later and, y'know, play a few songs with the band Vanessa's hired?'

'We certainly would not,' said Cass.

'Sorry,' said Alice. 'It's just ... we haven't practised anything. And, um, well, we don't want to.' Which, for Alice, is pretty blunt.

Sarah sighed. 'That's okay,' she said and, for a moment, I felt sorry for her. Imagine if your job meant travelling the world, looking for evil spoiled brats and then going to their mad birthday parties. It must be awful.

'Anyway,' said Sarah. 'I'm afraid you're all going to have to come in to the ballroom. We can't have any of the guests wandering around the house. It's an insurance thing.'

'We won't wander,' said Jane. 'We can just stay here.'

And we all nodded. Sarah sighed again.

'Sorry girls,' she said. 'It's the rule. Anyway,' she added more brightly, 'it'll be fun in there! You can dance with a fairytale prince!'

We just stared at her. I think she knew we were not the sort of girls who would find it fun to dance with someone who was being paid to be a fairytale prince. But she was right that we didn't have a choice. So we all got up and trooped across to the ballroom.

'By the way, is there going to be a pink pony?' said Cass. 'I've been looking forward to it.'

'You're getting obsessed with it, Cass,' said Alice.

'It's a pink pony! Vanessa's been going on about it for months! I just want to see it at last,' said Cass.

'A pony? Oh, yes,' said Sarah distractedly, looking at something on her clipboard. 'It'll be around later.'

'Well that's something,' said Cass. 'I suppose.'

A lot more happened after that but just thinking about it is exhausting. I am going to have to go to bed. Maybe it will all seem less mental in the morning.

SUNDAY

I am writing this in bed, still knackered after yesterday's party.

I don't know how all those celebrities who go out every night do it – especially the ones who drink a lot. I am a total wreck after just one day of serious partying AND of course there was no booze. I couldn't sleep in properly because my annoying family got up at the crack of dawn (nine o'clock) and because they have no consideration for others they went stomping about the house and put on the radio really loudly.

I tried to get my mother to bring me up some breakfast in bed, but she, of course, has no sympathy for my tired and emotional state.

'Well, you know what I think,' she said, when she eventually came upstairs in response to my plaintive cries for help. 'I think it was ridiculous to go in the first place.'

Though, because she is not a total monster, she was horrified to hear about what happened to poor Alice. But I haven't got to that yet. I'd better continue the terrible tale.

So yes, anyway, when we all went back into the ballroom, the party was in full swing. Everyone was whirling around the dancefloor, some with the princes, some with ordinary guests. The classical music had stopped and another band was playing chart hits. We tried to hide near the door in case any of the princes dragged us up on the dance floor. In fairness, plenty of our classmates seemed to be enjoying themselves. There was still glitter in the air, but Vanessa herself was nowhere to be seen. We grabbed some Cokes from a passing fairytale prince, who had apparently been relegated to drink-serving duty, and stayed in the background. It got a bit boring after a while because the music was too loud to talk properly. Then suddenly the music stopped and a man's deep voice boomed over the sound system.

'Everybody,' roared the mysterious voice, 'I want you all to give it up for Miss ... Vanessa ... Finn!'

'Oops,' said Jane. 'I've got to go. See you later.' And she disappeared into the crowd.

There was a blinding flash of light and a burst of smoke and Vanessa appeared on the podium, striking a dramatic pose. The glossy gang and the fairytale princes all started clapping and cheering (as did some of our class, who really should have known better). Then a fairytale prince walked up to each side of Vanessa and took her hand. As the band kicked into a brand new song, she strutted down from the podium and the glossy goons – and Jane – formed a group around her. And then we realised that the song was about Vanessa herself, and she and the goons (and Jane) were performing an elaborate dance routine to it!

I can't even describe how awful the song was. Bits of it were kind of spoken instead of sung and it went something like this:

Ah ... ah ... Vanessa!

Ah ... ah ... Vanessa!

Glamorous

Fabulous

A diva

Supreme

She's the girl the boys all want

And the girls all want to be

'That is the biggest lie I've ever heard in my life,' said Cass.

'Well, maybe boys do all want her,' said Alice. 'We've never asked any.'

'They may,' said Cass, 'though I can't understand why. But I bet there isn't a single girl on earth who actually wants to be her.'

'I dunno,' said Ellie. 'Look at Karen Rodgers.'

We looked over at Karen, who was still with the same fairytale prince who'd whisked her away earlier. She was gazing at Vanessa in awe and sort of shimmying along.

'Poor Jane,' said Alice. 'This must be the terrible surprise she couldn't tell us about.'

'She's very good,' I said. 'Jane, I mean. You'd never know how she was feeling inside.' She was doing the dance perfectly, smiling perkily all the while, even though we knew she didn't want to be there. Vanessa wasn't doing as much dancing as the others – she was mostly striking poses while the rest of the goons danced around her – but she did perform some quite complicated moves and I had to admit that she had a good sense of timing (as a drummer, I notice these things). Which didn't make up for the fact that the whole thing was completely ridiculous and terrible.

'This is the worst song ever,' said Cass. 'I wonder who wrote it?'

'Maybe she wrote it herself?' said Jessie. 'The lyrics, I mean.'

The song was still going on. It just got worse.

Ah ... ah ... Vanessa! Ah ... ah ... Vanessa!

She's a princess

She's a queen

She's an empress too

Everybody clap your hands

At Vanessa's birthday do

'How can she be a princess, a queen and an empress?' asked Ellie. 'That doesn't even make sense!'

'I know,' said Cass. 'And what is she meant to be the queen and the empress and the princess of? Not our class, I hope.'

The whole thing was terrible, but it was also sort of mesmerising. In fact, Alice and I climbed onto some chairs and stood on them so we could get a better view of the horrible sight.

At last the song ended, with all the dancers stretching their arms out to Vanessa while she posed triumphantly in the centre. Even more glitter fell from the ceiling then, which I would like to think is the only reason why everyone shrieked, and they weren't screaming with joy and admiration. Vanessa leapt gracefully back up on the podium in her sparkly heels (I've said it before and I'll say it again – for someone who generally wears very awkward footwear she is very nimble) and grabbed yet another microphone.

'Thank you, everyone!' she cried, as if we'd all been whooping and cheering and stamping our feet with joy. 'In a few minutes, I'm going to show how grateful I am to all of you for coming by singing a very special new song with this amazing band. But now it's time for a very special part of today's fabulous celebrations – the birthday cake!'

The door from the hall opened, some cameras moved in that direction, and something very peculiar came in.

'Oh my God,' said Cass, gleefully. 'It's here!'

It was the pony. It had clearly once been white (or grey, as white horses are mysteriously called. I don't know why), but now it was bright pink, apart from its mane, which was still pale silvery grey. It was surprisingly large – I mean, it wasn't a little cute Shetland pony. To be honest, I'd have thought it was a plain old horse. Anyway, it didn't look very happy, understandably enough. It was attached to a little pink cart on which was a giant tower of bright pink cupcakes. Everyone gasped.

'You know,' said Cass, who had got up on the chair next to me. 'In a way, this is just as insanely brilliant as I hoped it was going to be, but in another ... well, I dunno. The pony looks a bit cross. I hope it's okay.'

'Maybe it'll bite Vanessa,' said Ellie hopefully.

And actually, that's almost what happened. Some men came over and unhitched the cart from the pony as the cameras pointed at Vanessa, who was skipping over to pet it (the pony, not the cart). They moved the cart to the side and pulled down some glittering covers over the wheels so it looked like a fancy table. Lots of camera flashes started going off as people tried to take photos. The pony looked crosser and crosser and then, when Vanessa flung her arms around its neck so the camera crew could get a close up, it just lost its temper (who could blame it?) and sort of reared up. Vanessa shrieked and fell back, but unfortunately (for her, not for us – we found this all very entertaining) she fell right back into the cart/table. Which meant she fell right back into the giant pile of cupcakes, which tumbled to the ground along with Vanessa herself.

It was madness. Vanessa was lying there on a pile of squashed cakes, covered in more of the cakes, shrieking all the while and kicking her legs about. Meanwhile, the pony had made a bid for freedom and was trotting across the room at a scarily fast pace.

'Oh my God,' said Cass. 'It's heading our way! Come on!'

She jumped off her chair, and so did I, but it was like Alice was frozen. She just stood there, petrified, staring at the pony.

'Come on, Alice!' I shouted. And then she jumped. But she was in such a panic she didn't land properly. Instead, she sort of fell off the chair and crashed onto the ground.

Everyone screamed, including me, but Alice herself didn't. She just lay there looking very white and scared.

'Oh my God,' I said in horror. 'She's dead!'

'No I'm not,' said Alice, feebly. 'But ... ow! OW! I think ... ow ... I think something's happened to my wrist.' She tried to sit up as Sarah the producer pushed her way through the crowd (the pony, by the way, had been captured and taken out by its keepers. It looked very pleased with itself.). The cameras, I noticed, were still focused on Vanessa, who was trying to stand up but kept slipping on the cupcakes.

'Oh God, this is all we need,' muttered Sarah. 'No, don't move!' she said to Alice. 'We'll have to get an ambulance.'

'I don't think I need an ambulance,' said Alice. 'I mean, it's just my wrist.'

'Better safe than sorry,' said Sarah. 'I'll get the first-aid team anyway.' She helped Alice get up and sit in the chair she'd just fallen off.

By this stage, Vanessa was upright. She didn't seem to have hurt herself (probably because the cakes broke her fall). But she was, of course, in a rage. Sarah's assistant stayed with us as Sarah moved back to the camera crew. 'Keep shooting!' she cried. 'Vanessa, can you tell us how you're feeling?'

'How do you think I'm feeling!' screamed Vanessa, stamping a sparkly foot. She went on roaring at the camera while her minion Caroline nervously tried to tell her that everything wasn't that bad. I'm glad that she now knows the awfulness of falling over embarrassingly in public, after the fuss she made when I did it.

But I wasn't thinking about that at the time. I was just thinking about poor Alice. The first aider had checked her out and agreed that there didn't seem to be anything seriously wrong but that she should go to hospital straight away. So she was taken off in one of the crew's fancy jeep things to hospital while the rest of us just sat there.

'Do you think she'll be okay?' asked Cass, nervously.

'Well, they did say it was just her wrist,' I said. But still, that's bad enough. She did look very pale and stunned.

The party didn't last long after that. I think the TV people just wanted to get lots of footage of Vanessa going mad. The band didn't bother playing. The caterers brought out more trays of food so we all just hung around for an hour or so eating it and talking. Jane had found us after Alice was taken away and apologised for what she'd just taken part in.

'I had no choice,' she said. 'But you should know that I did want to get sick throughout.'

'So did we,' said Cass.

'I nearly did,' I said.

We exchanged numbers with Jane and promised to text her to tell her how Alice is. She suggested meeting up with her and her best friend from school some time, which would be cool. Then Sarah took up a microphone.

'Thanks so much, everyone, for coming to Vanessa's big birthday bash.'

'If you put this on TV, I'll sue!' shrieked Vanessa in the background.

Sarah turned to her and whispered, but loudly enough for the mike to pick it up, 'You can't, Vanessa, it's all in the contract.' She turned back to all of us. 'I have to remind you all that you can't post any photos or video from tonight online until after the show airs. That's all part of the agreement you and your parents signed. Anyway, the buses have arrived to take home the girls from St Dominic's and the theatre class. Have a good evening.'

We all started filing out of the house. As we did, the camera crew started coming around to people and asking them to tell them what we thought of the party.

'Ooh,' said Cass. 'I hope they come up to us.'

And then they did.

'So girls,' said a producer. 'This was quite a party, right? Can you tell us what you thought of it? And can you speak in complete sentences – like, say "This party was great" rather than "It was great"? So, tell us all about it.'

And, for a moment, I thought, 'Aha, this is my chance to get my own back for the way Vanessa behaved when my mum's book came out and the time she screamed at me at the Battle of the Bands!' But I don't know what came over us because we couldn't do it. Neither of us could. To say something, I dunno, snide about her on telly when we had, after all, come to her party and she'd just been totally humiliated at that party just seemed ... too mean. Thousands of people would see it.

I know I don't like Vanessa, and I know we just came to her birthday bash because we thought it would be mental, and I know we bitch about her in school, and I know she had no problem with humiliating me in public herself, but laughing at her on telly just didn't feel right. It felt properly bitchy. Afterwards, Cass told me that she felt the same way.

So I just said, 'I've never been to a party like this one.'

And Cass said, 'This party was very spectacular.'

And that was it. We said bye to Jane and got on the bus.

When we had sat down, I said, 'You know, we just got the

chance to have public revenge on Vanessa for all the times she's been rude to us and we didn't take it. I think we must be much better people than I thought we were. That was pretty good of us, wasn't it?'

'I think if we were properly good we wouldn't even think of that,' said Cass, and she's probably right. But still. I think it was quite saintly of us.

The bus journey home was quite different from the journey there. We were all kind of knackered and we'd spent the last bit of the party just hanging around. So there was no singing. Ellie and Jessie talked a bit about the musical auditions. Ellie really wants to work with Mrs Limond, who is this old lady who used to be an art teacher at our school and who returns every year to oversee the costumes. We have never met her, but she is famous because apparently she is a bit eccentric and mysterious. We have seen her costumes, though, because we were at the musical last year (and I went to see Rachel's year's production before I started at our school) and they are actually amazing. Anyway, normally I'd have been quite interested in what Ellie was saying because, after all, mysterious old ladies who make magical costumes are always interesting, but I felt like I'd sort of crashed down to earth after the madness and excitement of the party. So I just sat there and stared at the window and said 'Oh?' every so often in what I hope was an interested voice.

Anyway, that was Vanessa's party. I can't believe it ended up with Alice in hospital. She texted me last night to say she was still waiting in A&E, but they don't think there's anything seriously wrong. I haven't heard from her this morning yet. I suppose she's sleeping in, like I'd be if I didn't have the loudest family on earth.

No mail from Paperboy, by the way. But, at the moment, I'm almost too tired to care.

LATER

Terrible news. It turns out Alice fractured her left wrist. She will be in a cast for weeks! She says it doesn't hurt, but she is still feeling a bit wobbly. Poor Alice. Hurting her left wrist is particularly annoying – it means she can't get out of school work because she can still write, but she can't play the guitar because she can't hold down the strings to make different chords (if it was her right wrist she'd still be able to strum the strings with her right hand).

And of course me and Cass are affected too. Because without Alice on guitar, there can be no more Hey Dollface until she gets better. No more band practices. No more venting my feelings by bashing the drums (I can use the sofa and cushions like I used to when I was just starting, but it's not the same now I'm really used to playing the real things). I mean, I suppose I could go out to Alice's house anyway and play them there, but it wouldn't really be fair to Alice to play drums in her house (well, next to her house) while she can't play anything. So no more drumming for weeks. No more of that brilliant feeling when a song works out. And just when I was determined to get everything back to normal between the three of us! How will I stick to my new rule about doing stuff and bonding now?

Nothing is going right this week.

There is one bright side, though. I texted Jane to tell her about Alice and she texted back to say that Mrs Finn came in to Jane's mum today, and Jane heard her say she thinks Vanessa has gone too far and that maybe they have been spoiling her too much. At last! Maybe this means Vanessa will not spend her next birthday doing what she did last year, ie boasting loudly about how expensive her presents were and how her new bag cost more than she bets our parents earn in a week (she was probably right, but how obnoxious and silly). I hope the Finn parents' reign of strictness has kicked in by tomorrow otherwise Vanessa will be even worse than ever now that she has been thwarted by the 'Big Birthday Bash' people.

MONDAY

I'm not sure whether the reign of strictness has begun or not. Vanessa doesn't seem to have changed at all. She spent most of today boasting about how wonderful her party was, as if we all hadn't been there and seen everything (including, of course, the pony running amok and knocking her into a pile of cupcakes).

'In a way,' said Cass, as we watched Vanessa holding forth to Caroline and Karen Rodgers and Alison on the other side of the classroom, 'you've got to admire her. I mean, she doesn't let things get to her, does she?'

'But in another way,' said Ellie, 'that kind of shows she's a psychopath.'

'True,' said Cass. 'You wouldn't know she'd been knocked into some cakes by a pink pony. While covered in glitter.'

'And she's even got some new fans out of the whole thing,'

said Ellie. 'Look, Karen and Alison seem to like her now.'

'That's because Karen snogged that fairytale prince,' said Emma.

And we all screamed 'What?!' because none of us had heard about this on Saturday night, probably because we all more worried about Alice than Karen Rodgers's love life. But Emma was talking to Alison at the lockers this morning (they are both going to the new computer classes that are starting next week) and apparently it was true. The fairytale princes were all boys from some local drama club and Karen had danced with the same boy all night and ended up kissing him among the bean bags. And he took her number and texted her yesterday and they're meeting up at the weekend.

'Maybe love will change Karen,' said Cass. 'Maybe it'll make her nicer.'

'Hmmm,' I said. 'The only thing that's ever made her a tiny bit nicer was Alison finally standing up to her at the Battle of the Bands.'

'I wish Alison had got together with a fairytale prince instead of Karen,' said Cass, and we all agreed with her. 'She deserves it much more. Not that that prince is my type at all.'

'His name is Bernard,' said Emma. 'Alison told me. It's not

really a very prince-y name, is it?'

'In fairness,' said Jessie, 'he did actually look quite fairytale prince-ish. I mean, he wasn't my type either. He was really cheesy-looking. But he looked quite, you know. Glamorous.'

'Karen Rodgers has a glamorous fairytale prince,' said Cass. 'And meanwhile poor Alice has a fractured wrist. Life isn't fair.'

It really isn't. As yet more proof that they have forgotten how miserable I am, Mum and Dad made me peel about ten million potatoes for dinner tonight. It felt like that many, anyway, but Mum said I was being ridiculous and there were only five potatoes. She also said that when she was a kid she had to help make dinner every single day and that me and Rachel were spoiled rotten in comparison. Dad said that he thought peeling potatoes was fun which was a barefaced lie because it clearly is not. And as I said to him, if it was so much fun then why didn't he do it tonight? But he said he had essays to correct. Huh.

LATER

I am still writing poetry to deal with my general angst. It is quite cathartic, really. I feel quite proud of myself for rhyming

'Far away in Vancouver' with 'I am forced to hoover'. It shows the contrast between Paperboy's glamorous exile and my horrible life as a lonely domestic servant.

TUESDAY ☾

I have had an amazing brainwave. I know how me and Cass and Alice can bond again. We're going to be in a musical. I don't mean we're going to, like, start singing in the streets like loons. Or put a musical on ourselves. No, we can be in the school musical!

My great idea came to me this morning in Room 7. It was an English class. Mrs Harrington was going on about some poem or other (luckily she has more or less stopped going on about my mother's books all the time. I think the novelty of having Rosie Carberry's daughter in her class has worn off at last, thank God). Anyway, even when she is not being incredibly annoying she is very boring so I was looking off into space and suddenly I realised that I was staring at the class noticeboard. And that's when I saw the notice about the musical auditions. Obviously I had seen it before as it had been up for weeks, and Jessie and Ellie have been talking about the auditions for a while, but this time it was like a lightbulb went on and I had my brilliant idea. What could be a more perfect way of getting us all to spend proper bonding time together than doing the musical? Apart from, I dunno, going on holiday together, which isn't very practical in February.

And the thing is, if we try out for the musical we'll definitely get to do something because it's just for our year. Every year a different year gets to put on the show (it used to be open to the whole school, but the fifth and sixth years kept getting all the decent parts, which wasn't very fair, so now they move it around so everyone gets a chance at some stage) and this year it's the second year's turn. The school collaborates with St Anthony's down the road so some BOYS get to take part too, but it was our school's idea so it's mostly us. They only get a few boys in to do a couple of the really deep parts and do some heavy lifting.

I hadn't thought about it much this year because I was so caught up in my woe (and to be honest I would rather have been going to band practice after school than prancing about with my classmates in the school hall). But now there is (a) no band practice for weeks until Alice gets better and (b) I have to try and stop being so miserable all the time. So it seems like the perfect thing to do. We'd be spending time together working on a new project. I would be too busy learning dances or making sets to worry about Paperboy and my terrible life. It will help me stick to several rules at once! And the auditions are on Thursday.

I told Cass and Alice about my amazing scheme as soon as the class was finished (I didn't tell them that I thought we needed to bond. They might think that was a bit weird. So I said it would be a fun thing to do while the band is on a break). Cass is actually really into the idea. I was kind of surprised by this (it took ages to persuade her to actually start the band and then do the Battle) until she told me that she didn't want to perform in it, she wanted to work backstage.

'At last,' she cried, 'I can live out my dream of being a set designer.'

I have to admit that I had totally forgotten it was her dream to be a set designer, which isn't surprising because, as I pointed out the last time we talked about this, she never really goes to the theatre so I don't know why she feels so strongly about designing sets. But she does, so there you go. Anyway, whether we're backstage or on stage, we'll still all be involved, so that is fine.

Alice was slightly less enthusiastic. I think falling off a chair has made her a bit less cheerful, which is understandable I suppose.

'I can't do anything with my plaster,' she said miserably.

'But why?' I said. 'I mean, you can sing. And it's *Mary Poppins*! It's not like it's one of those musicals where you have to do, like, breakdancing and stuff.'

I'm not totally sure if there actually are any musicals where you have to do breakdancing. But there probably are.

'Hmmm,' said Alice.

'Or you could work backstage,' I suggested. 'Like Cass. She wants to design the sets.'

'Oh yes,' said Alice. 'I'd forgotten about the set thing.'

'So had I,' I said. 'Actually, I thought she had too. But she hasn't. Anyway, if you don't feel like singing you can do that! Or look after the sound or something. Whatever you like.'

'But my plaster ...' began Alice.

'Your right arm is fine!' I said. 'Which is what you do most work with. Apart from the guitar of course. But, in fairness, there isn't much chance of anyone playing the guitar in *Mary Poppins*.'

'I suppose not,' said Alice. 'So what exactly do you want to do? In the musical, I mean.'

'Well,' I said, 'I don't know, really. I'll probably be in the chorus.' I paused. 'Though of course, there's always Mary Poppins herself ...'

Alice made a peculiar noise that sounded a little bit like a laugh but can't have been because she said, very seriously, 'That's a good idea but ... don't you need more experience?'

'Well, no one in our class has experience,' I said.

'As far as we know,' said Alice. 'Everyone's full of surprises recently. Think of Karen and the fairytale prince!'

'Good point,' I said.

'And we don't know much about the girls in other classes in our year. I mean, for all we know, Susie Murray is a ... a prima ballerina!'

Susie Murray is in 2:1 and is in my German class. She could actually be a ballerina for all I know, I've never talked to her about anything besides how to get to an imaginary train station in Frankfurt.

'Also a good point,' I said. 'But still, she probably isn't. I mean, everyone has a chance at an open audition. Don't they?'

'Yeah,' said Alice.

'But,' I said honestly, 'I'll probably just be in the chorus. If I'm lucky.'

Alice said, 'Oh no, there's a chance you'll get a big part,' but she wasn't very convincing. Still, the chorus will still be fun, won't it? I mean, it's still show business. Sort of. So we're all going to try and take part in the musical. It's not the same as band stuff, but at least it's something. And it might distract me from thinking about how Paperboy has forgotten all about me. Which he has. Still no mail.

WEDNESDAY

I have been practising my song for the musical. I am going to sing the lullaby from *Mary Poppins*. My mum used to sing it to us when we were little, so I know it really well. Mary Poppins gets the children to go to sleep by singing them a song about staying awake, and it's quite a nice tune, really. Of course, my selfish family is not supportive of my new dream. Rachel stomped into my room in her usual charming style just when I was getting going.

'Oh my God,' she said. 'It was bad enough when you were drumming on saucepans. But if you're going to start shrieking and wailing too, I'm going to have to move out.'

'I was practising for the school musical auditions!' I said.

'It's tomorrow!'

'Since when did you want to be in the musical?' said Rachel.

I nearly said 'Since Tuesday', but instead said, 'I've always been interested in the theatre.'

Rachel snorted like the pig she is.

'Huh,' she said. 'That's news to me. What part are you going for?'

'I dunno,' I said. 'I mean, I'll probably just be in the chorus.'

I keep saying that, but secretly I have been hoping that I'll get a proper part. I mean, my singing isn't too bad. And I know I can act. I used to want to be an actress and I've always thought I could do it quite well if I tried. And I went to speech and drama for a while too, and I was pretty good. I especially liked doing improvisations, where you make up a story and act it out. And when I was younger I used to read out bits of the dialogue from books I liked (just in my room when no one can hear me) and, if I say so myself, my acting is quite powerful. I used to read out a bit of *A Little Princess* (which is a very sad book about a poor orphan girl) and I almost made myself cry. So I must be able to act a bit.

Also, Mum was a member of her college drama society ten million years ago (in the '80s) and they went over to do some big student drama festival in London once. So the theatre is in my blood. Sort of. I think I might have a chance, anyway. It's not like anyone else in my class is known for her great theatrical skills. I figure that if I can sing in tune, I have as good a chance as anyone else.

Anyway, Rachel said, 'Well, that's quite fun. Jenny was in the chorus when our year did it and she said it was a great laugh.'

'Didn't you do the sets or something?' I said. 'That's what Cass wants to do.'

'I did,' she said. 'And that's where I met Tom.'

I had totally forgotten that that was how she'd met her boyfriend. They've been going out for so long (well, two years), it feels like they've been together forever.

'Oh my God,' I said. 'So you did. What was he doing?'

'Carrying giant lights around,' said Rachel.

'Because of his manly strength and huge muscles?' I said, and sniggered. Because Tom is quite good looking but he is also rather skinny. In a nice way, I should add. Rachel knew I was only joking because, instead of screaming at me, she just threw a pillow at me.

'Exactly,' she said. She looked all wistful. If we were in a film, everything would have gone all wobbly and black and white and there'd have been a flashback to two years ago in our school hall. 'I was painting a cardboard table and he nearly knocked my paint pot over with a giant light.'

'How romantic,' I said.

'It was, actually,' said Rachel. She looked at me in a serious big sisterly way. This was never good.

'You know, you might meet someone yourself on the musical,' she said, in a careful sort of voice.

'Why,' I said, 'would I want to do that?'

'Well ... you know,' said Rachel. 'I mean, it's months since Paperboy ... went away. And, you know, it might be ages before you see him again ...'

'I don't care!' I cried. 'I don't want to meet anyone else!'

And I don't. I know I might never see Paperboy again, but it doesn't make any difference. I still miss him. I don't care about other boys. I can't believe Rachel thinks I'm so shallow.

'I bet if Tom went off to Canada, you wouldn't run off with the first boy who ... who tripped over your paint pot!' I said.

Rachel sighed in an annoying, grown-up way.

'No,' she said. 'But after a while ... well, you know, people break up and go out with other people all the time ...'

Just hearing her say that about breaking up made me want to burst into tears. But I didn't. I just sniffed.

'We haven't broken up,' I said.

'Oh,' said Rachel. 'Okay. Anyway, I'm going to ring Tom. Can you keep the noise down?'

'No,' I said, childishly.

Rachel sighed again. 'Well, try.' And off she went. I felt rotten. I know that me and Paperboy haven't broken up, but are you really going out with someone who hasn't bothered to contact you in weeks and weeks? I don't know if you are.

Anyway, I can't think about it now. I must practise my song again. And if it disturbs Rachel's conversation with her precious Tom, then GOOD.

LATER

I told Mum about the musical and she was surprisingly encouraging about it for someone whose usual mission seems to be to destroy all my hopes and dreams. And listen to this: she told me that she was not only in the college drama society, but in third year she was also in the musical society, and so was Dad! In fact, they did a musical together! I knew the theatre was in my blood.

'It was a lot of fun,' she said. 'We did *The Pirates of Penzance*. I must dig out the photos.'

The last thing I would normally want to see is a load of pictures of my parents poncing about in tights, but now I am planning to be a musical star I need all the background information I can get.

'Did you have a proper part?' I asked.

'Well yeah,' said Mum. It turns out she was the Pirate King, which is the biggest part of all! I asked why a girl was playing the Pirate King and she said they were a very open-minded musical society.

'A group of us women said it wasn't fair that the men always got all the best parts and the girls just had to stand around being soppy, so they decided to open it up a bit,' she said fondly. 'It was great fun. I got to swing around the stage on a rope.'

I wanted to find out more about Mum's youthful stardom but I have to practise a bit more first. Still, now it looks like she will be able to give me lots of advice on becoming a musical star. Who knew my mother could actually have a positive effect on my life? I didn't think this was possible.

Still no mail from you-know-who. But I don't really have time to worry about it. I need to do more practising now.

FRIDAY ☺

I don't believe it. I do NOT believe it. I already knew the world wasn't fair, but now I have proof. The cast was announced today. And there is truly no justice in the universe because I still can't believe who got the lead role.

I was feeling quite optimistic before the auditions at lunchtime yesterday. Everyone who wanted to sing and dance on stage had to go to the school hall and everyone who wanted to work backstage went to language lab. So I headed off to the hall with Jessie and Alice (she has decided to try for the chorus too, which makes sense because, to be honest, she can sing better than I can) while Cass and Ellie went to offer their services designing sets and costumes and whatnot. You had to write your name on a list when you came in so we did that and then took a seat to wait for our names to be called.

I was kind of surprised by who was there. Karen and Alison, for example. Maybe falling in love with a fairytale prince (called Bernard) has transformed Karen in all sorts of ways. And Vanessa was there, looking as smug as ever.

'Wow, nothing can stop her,' said Jessie. 'Not even being pushed over by a pony. She's like an old-fashioned diva. Or an evil robot.'

'Maybe going to that music, dance and whatever class has gone to her head,' I said. 'And now she thinks she really is talented.'

'Well, maybe she is,' said Alice. 'I mean, she could be. We've never actually heard her sing. Or seen her act. And remember, she was going to sing with the band last night before the whole angry pony thing.'

'That doesn't prove anything,' I said. 'Even if Vanessa couldn't sing, she wouldn't let it stop her from showing off.'

'True,' said Jessie, and then Ms Byrne, the English teacher who always organises the school show, walked onto the hall's stage. I wish she was our English teacher, she seems much more normal than Mrs Harrington

'Welcome, second years!' she said cheerfully. 'I hope you're all very excited about this year's wonderful musical. I know you're all going to be great, so let's get started. You're all going to sing a bit of a song you've prepared, and then we're going to act out a bit of a scene together. Okay? And don't worry if you don't get a big part – there'll be room for everyone else in the chorus.'

Vanessa looked even more pleased with herself than ever, as if she already knew she was going to get a big part. Which, in fairness, turned out to be true. Unfortunately.

'Right, said Ms Byrne. 'The first up is ... Karen Rodgers!' Karen grinned nervously at Alison in a way that made her look like an actual human being as opposed to a mean bitch who likes mocking other girls for what their annoying mothers do.

'What are you going to sing, Karen?' asked Ms Byrne, as Karen took to the stage.

'"Don't Stop Believin",' said Karen.

I have to admit that I was hoping she'd be terrible. I mean, she'd been so awful to me when my mum's book came out that I was looking forward to seeing her make a fool of herself. But I didn't get my wish, because she wasn't bad at all. And then Ms Byrne gave her the script and they acted out a few lines and she was quite good at that too. I was shocked. When she finished Ms Byrne looked pleased and said 'Very good, Karen, you've got us off to a great start.'

Then a girl from 2:3 called Katie went up and sang 'Tomorrow' and on it went. I started to get more and more nervous. Loads of the girls could sing pretty well, and some of them were really good actors too. It started to dawn on me that I mightn't have a chance of getting even a tiny speaking part. Alice sang very well, as usual, and Ms Byrne assured her that if she wanted to be in the chorus her plaster wasn't a problem.

Then Jessie was called up and sang 'Who Will Buy This Wonderful Morning?' from *Oliver*. But I barely noticed her acting because she had written her name down just before me which meant that I was next. And it seemed like just a second later that I heard Ms Byrne saying 'Very good, Miss King. Now, Rebecca Rafferty, you're up next.'

The good thing about being in a band is that even though we've only played one gig, I'm not as nervous about getting up on a stage as I used to be. I mean, after you've fallen off a drum stool in front of a huge crowd of people, nothing can really faze you. So when I found myself actually up on the stage, I sort of stopped feeling nervous and just sang the lullaby from *Mary Poppins* as well as I could. Which was quite well, if I say so myself. The theatre is in my blood, after all. Then Ms Byrne gave me the script. It was the scene where Mary Poppins tells the kids that she's practically perfect in every way. I had to do a few lines as Mary and a few as one of the kids. And that was it. I was feeling quite pleased, and Jessie whispered to me that I'd done really well. But I didn't get to say thanks because Vanessa was striding confidently onto the stage as though she were a big star and we'd all been waiting for her.

'Hi, everyone!' she said, before Ms Byrne could say anything. 'I'm going to sing "Memories" from *Cats*.'

Alice, Jessie and I looked at each other and rolled our eyes. Jessie is good at doing this because she is long-sighted and her glasses make her eyes look slightly bigger than they actually are.

'Well, this'll be good,' said Jessie.

But it really was. As soon as Vanessa started to sing our jaws literally dropped open. Because she could sing. I mean *really* sing. And not in a bellowing, X-Factor sort of way. She had what my mum always calls a 'pure' voice – I mean she didn't sound like she was showing off at all. It was just a lovely clear sound. It was SO not how I expected Vanessa to sing. When she finished I found myself clapping automatically. THAT'S how good she was.

'Oh my God,' said Jessie, who'd also clapped, without

thinking, as had Alice. 'I can't believe we just applauded Vanessa. Voluntarily.'

I was thinking the same thing, but I couldn't say so because now Vanessa was acting a scene with Ms Byrne and she was really good at that too. She wasn't annoying or smug at all, which just shows that she really is a good actress. She was all bright and brisk and Mary Poppins-ish. It was amazing. And very, very irritating. She was by far the best in the whole group. When everyone had had their audition Ms Byrne thanked us all and told us that what she called 'a preliminary cast list' would be posted on the noticeboard outside the library at the end of the school day. Ellie, Alice and I trudged out of the hall and off to SS2, where we were having geography. Vanessa strutted past us, looking even more pleased with herself than usual (which is saying something). She was with Karen and Alison. Karen was telling her how brilliant her voice was. That's all we need, Karen and Vanessa teaming up.

When we arrived at geography, Cass and Ellie were in great form.

'I'm going to help Ms Dowling do the sets!' said Cass.

'And I'm working on the costumes,' said Ellie. 'But Mrs Limond wasn't there, which was a bit disappointing. I want to see if she really has purple hair. How was the audition?'

So we told them about Vanessa.

'She can't have been that good,' said Cass. 'I just refuse to believe it.'

'She was,' I said. 'I even clapped for her.'

'So did I,' said Jessie, 'without thinking, of course.'

'I hate to say this,' said Alice, 'but I think she's going to get the lead. I mean, she was the best.'

And as it turned out, Alice was right. When the list went up this morning, there she was at the top! Vanessa is Mary Poppins! And if that weren't bad enough, Karen Rodgers is Michael, one of the children. And if THAT weren't bad enough, I am her understudy. Yes, I am understudying Karen Rodgers to play a small boy. I am starting to think that this was not such a good idea after all. So much for my musical genes.

On the (tiny) plus side, Jessie got a proper part, playing the cook. And Cass and Alice are all excited about the whole thing now, so part of my plan is working already – we have an exciting new project that has nothing to do with paperboys or me moping (not that I will admit to doing that) at all. So that's something. Oh, and Susie Murray from 2:1 is playing Mrs Banks, the children's mother. It turns out she is quite talented after all.

So anyway, the first rehearsal is after school on Monday. We all had to gather in the hall at lunchtime today and Ms Byrne gave us each a CD of the songs along with a script and told us to study both of them carefully over the weekend so we're familiar with the story and the songs. I just hope Karen and Vanessa aren't too irritating at the first big rehearsal (though I am sure they will be).

Still no mail from Paperboy. I am starting to get angry as well as sad.

SATURDAY ☺

I told Mum (and Dad) about just being in the chorus. They acted like this was a great thing.

'Being in the chorus is lots of fun,' said Dad. 'You get the excitement of being in the show and none of the stress!'

'He's right,' said Mum. 'There were loads of times in *The Pirates of Penzance* when I would have loved to just be in the chorus. Having a big part isn't all fun, you know.'

'Remember that time you stabbed Dave Scully with your sword by mistake?' said Dad. 'He had to go to hospital and everything!'

'It wasn't a real sword,' said Mum. 'He was just bruised.'

'I don't think there'd be any chance of me stabbing someone by accident in *Mary Poppins*,' I said. But I saw her point. Maybe it is for the best that I don't have a big part to worry about? I'm in quite a fragile state at the moment; my nerves probably couldn't take it.

LATER

Although in that case, I am not sure my nerves will be able to take the sight of Vanessa being all smug as the star of the show. Hmmm.

SUNDAY ☼

Very boring weekend. I ended up spending most of it lying on my bed listening to the *Mary Poppins* soundtrack (really very catchy) and reading onc of my library books, *My Family and Other Animals* by Gerald Durrell, which is a true story about a boy who goes off to Corfu with his family and adopts loads of cool animals. His older siblings are totally head-wrecking, especially his pretentious big brother Larry, which is partly why I like it. But I also like it because I too have an affinity with the animal kingdom, as proved by the fact that every time I go to Alice's house in the country I always see loads of wild creatures. Well, squirrels. But they're wild, aren't they?

Of course, my sensible way of spending the weekend didn't please my tyrannical parents. Their sympathy for my relegation to the chorus didn't last very long. This afternoon my mother came in to my room (without knocking, of course. She has the manners of a ... I dunno. Something rude) when I was quietly reading, took one look at me and said, 'What on earth are you doing like that?'

'I am reading, mother,' I said. 'Isn't that obvious?'

'But why are you lying with your head over one side of the bed and the book on the floor? That can't be comfortable. Or good for your neck.'

Honestly! She can even find fault with the way I read! I don't even know why I was lying like that; it just felt like the right way to lie. Also it meant that when I needed to take a break from *Mary Poppins* I could reach over and change the music on my iPod which was plugged into its little speakers on a shelf by the bed. So I told her this and she said, 'Well, if you get a terrible crick in your neck, don't say I didn't warn you.'

And then she demanded I come down soon and chop up some carrots. Yet again, I wonder what the fans of my mother's books would think if they knew she made her children slave for her like skivvies. She and my dad are obsessed with making me and Rachel chop vegetables. When I grow up I'm never going to chop or peel anything. I'm going to live entirely on things you can just bite straight into, without doing anything, like apples. Unless, of course, I become incredibly rich. Then I'll have servants to make all my food for me.

Speaking of my evil mother, she is still writing a sequel to the terrible Ruthie nightmare. She promises that when it comes out she will make it very clear that Ruthie and her awful friends have nothing in common with me and Rachel. I hope she sticks to her word. I never thought I'd say this, but I really wish she'd just go back to writing books for grown-ups about twinkly-eyed kindly Irish mammies who solve all their family's problems (these books are clearly even more unlike her own family than the Ruthie one).

Okay, so I didn't like Mrs Harrington going on about them, but at least there was no chance of anyone thinking any of the characters have anything to do with me, given that I don't like Irish dancing and I don't live in a cottage. Lots of Mum's characters live in cosy cottages in quaint little villages. I don't know why, considering she's from Phibsboro and has never spent more than a week in a cottage in her life, and that was just on holiday.

Anyway, the main reason I spent most of my weekend at home reading and hoovering and dusting and chopping things like a servant is because Alice is off visiting relations (she spends loads of weekends doing this because (a) she is an only child and (b) half her relations are in Germany, so her parents are very keen on making sure she sees all her Irish relatives on a regular basis. So every few weekends she's dragged off to see some aunt or cousin or someone). And Cass was off with Liz from Bad Monkey. I am still worried that my misery and sorrow have driven away Cass and she has found a new joint-best-friend. I really hope not. I will just have to stick to my new rules and hope it all works out.

Although I sort of have a new friend as well. I texted Jane about Vanessa. Actually, I basically said, 'Why didn't you tell us she could sing?!' Jane rang me and we talked for quite a while. She is very nice and funny. She said she thought we all knew Vanessa could sing and I had to admit that Vanessa might well have boasted about her singing before. She goes on about how brilliant she is so much that we all kind of tune her out.

Anyway, strangely enough, it turns out Jane's school did *Mary Poppins* last year and she played Mr Banks, the children's father.

'I'm actually about six inches shorter than the girl who played Michael,' she said. 'So it looked a bit weird. But I think it worked.'

She said that she had a lot of fun in the musical and her friends were in the chorus and had a great time, so what with this and my parents' words of wisdom I feel a bit better now about being stuck in the boring old chorus while Vanessa and Karen Rodgers are the stars of the show.

Right, I'm going to go back to Gerald Durrell and *Mary Poppins*. It is quite a soothing combination. Which I need because there's still nothing from Paperboy. I'm not going to check my mail or Facebook until tomorrow, it's all stressing me out too much.

MONDAY

So, it turns out being in a musical is not what I expected. I thought it would be all just, you know, singing and dancing and improvising (my natural skill). But for now it seems to be all about something called 'stagecraft' (which as far as I can tell seems to mean 'walking across a stage without falling over') and being in what is essentially a choir! It is not very dramatic, at least if you're in the boring old chorus. But it was still quite fun, at least some of the time. Especially for Alice.

This is what happened. All us exciting glamorous musical people had to gather in the hall after last class.

'At last,' said Cass, as we walked down the corridor. 'My career as a set designer begins.'

'Are you actually going to be designing the sets?' said Alice. 'I mean, I think Ms Dowling might be doing the design part and you'll be doing the, I dunno, painting-bits-of-cardboard part. I don't know if you should get your hopes up ...'

But Cass said that she knew she was learning her new trade from the ground up.

'I have to start somewhere,' she said, which was worryingly sensible of her.

Ellie will be learning new skills too, from the mysterious Mrs Limond.

And I will be learning new skills as well, such as trying not to kill Karen Rodgers (this is going to be very difficult, as you will see).

When we got to the hall, the boys from St Anthony's were there already. To be honest, I'd kind of forgotten they were going to be doing the musical with us. But we saw them as soon as we walked into the hall, and I froze. So did Cass and Alice. Because there, sitting on a plastic chair in the St Dominic's school hall, all ready to play Bert the chimney sweep himself, was Bike Boy! Or Richard Murray, as he is really called.

'Oh my God,' said Cass. 'Is that who I think it is?'

'Bike Boy!' I said.

We both looked at Alice. She was just staring at Bike Boy and her cheeks had gone very pink. Then Bike Boy glanced over and saw us. He looked quite surprised too, but in a good way, I think. He smiled and raised his hand in greeting, so we sort of waved back.

'Where will we go? What will we do?' said Alice in a flustered way.

'Everyone's just sitting down,' said Cass. 'I don't think it matters where. Come on.'

Ellie had got there before us so we sat down next to her just as Ms Dowling (the art teacher) and Ms Byrne came in with a strange woman whom we'd never seen before. She was quite young and quite pretty in a dramatic sort of way. She had very dark shoulder-length hair with a very nice glossy fringe (I know it seems like I'm obsessed with other people's fringes, but it's because I can't have a decent fringe myself. I got one last year and it just grew straight out from my head in a mad way rather than falling down all shiny. Luckily, it grew out fairly quickly and even my hairdresser agreed it was a bad idea so as soon as it was long enough she just trimmed the edges so it went back into the rest of my hair. This was unlike poor old Cass, who's been trying to grow hers out for ages. Her hairdresser keeps cutting it back in).

Anyway, as well as her fringe, the mysterious woman was wearing a black and white stripy top, a black cardigan, black skinny jeans and black converse. She had lovely glowing skin and her lipstick was bright red. It looked like she wasn't wearing any other make-up but I had a feeling she was like my mum's friends who wear loads of really expensive make-up in order to look like they're not wearing any.

'Who's she?' said Ellie, who didn't recognise Bike Boy so wasn't as stunned as me, Cass and Alice. 'She looks kind of French.'

But she wasn't French. She and Ms Byrne and Ms Dowling, who is looking after the backstage stuff, went up on the stage.

'Hi everyone,' said Ms Byrne. 'Welcome to the first rehearsal of the second-year musical! Now, I'd like to introduce you to the director of this year's show. She's an up-and-coming director and a graduate of the Trinity College Drama department who happens to be a former St Dominic's girl. So please welcome Cathy Laverty.'

We all applauded politely and Ms Byrne passed the microphone to Cathy Laverty, who clearly wasn't French after all.

'Hi,' she said and looked out at us in an intense way. She has very big eyes. 'I'm Cathy Laverty, but you can all call me Cathy. And I'd like to welcome you all to a journey to the heart of *Mary Poppins*. You might think we're about to put on just another school musical ...' We all looked nervously at each other because to be honest, that is exactly what we thought. 'But,' Cathy (as we were told to call her) went on, 'we're embarking on an adventure in theatre.'

Heavens.

Cathy started talking about how we were setting off on a journey to the supercalifragilisticexpialidocious heart of *Mary Poppins*, and while this was going on I sneaked a glance at

Bike Boy (I should really start calling him Richard) and his cohorts. There were only a few of them and they all looked quite ordinary, apart from one tall, thin boy who was sitting next to Richard.

He had dark hair cut short at the back and sides but sort of floppy on top, like the First World War soldiers in Rachel's history book (the other week I was so bored by my own homework I wandered into Rachel's room and started flicking through her books to see if anything more exciting is awaiting me in a few years. It isn't). He wasn't exactly incredibly good-looking but he had an interesting face. And he wasn't listening to the speech either. In fact, he was reading a book. I couldn't see what it was at first, but it was a very battered-looking paperback that looked as if it had been published long before we were born.

I was still looking at him (while trying not to make it obvious that was I was looking at him) when Cathy finished her impassioned speech and gave the mike back to Ms Byrne, who thanked her and urged us to give her a welcoming round of applause. Which we did.

'And of course,' she said, when the clapping had stopped, 'we want to give a special St Dominic's welcome to our visitors from St Anthony's. Can we all welcome them with another big round of applause!'

We all clapped. Most of the boys looked slightly terrified for some reason, apart from Bike Boy, who looked like he was going to start laughing, and the tall, thin boy, who just kept reading his book, with an amused sort of expression on his face, as if a whole room full of girls weren't staring at him and clapping.

'Now,' Ms Byrne went on. 'Can I get the chorus over here, please? Principals, I want you over there with Cathy. Backstage crew, Ms Dowling will see you all up on the stage. Thanks, girls. And boys, of course.'

We all got up and shuffled over to our different groups. Cass kept looking significantly over to Bike Boy as she went up to the stage. Luckily, he didn't notice because he was coming our way.

'Hey,' he said, smiling at us as if were really pleased to see us (or at least Alice). 'Long time no see!'

'Hi,' said Alice. 'Um, how's your band?'

'Oh, fine,' said Bike Boy. 'Y'know. We're playing a gig soon. How's yours?'

'Sort of on hiatus at the moment,' said Alice, and lifted up her hand so he could see the plaster. Bike Boy whistled in a sympathetic way. But before he could say anything Ms Byrne called, 'I need all the chorus over here right now!' So we had to run over to her. But before we did, Bike Boy said, 'See you later!' And Alice went pinker than ever.

That's when I thought we'd get started on all the singing and dancing, but no! It was all about this stagecraft business, so us chorus people all had to gather at the back of a pretend stage (a corner of the hall) while Cathy Laverty showed the main actors where to stand and how to move about the stage while reading lines. Basically, it seemed to be about making sure they didn't have their backs turned to the audience half the time.

Vanessa was tossing her hair about (she must have learned some new tricks from her orange party pals) and looking disgustingly smug. And Karen wasn't much better. In fact, she was almost worse because she kept sucking up to Cathy.

'Oooh, Cathy, is this right?' she said in a simpering voice and I actually thought I was going to be sick. But that probably wouldn't have gone down very well with Cathy so I just made a sick face at Alice instead.

Anyway, even thought it was a bit boring standing there

in the background watching the stars of the show, it was also interesting at times because Bike Boy and the mysterious First World War boy, who turned out to be playing Mr Banks, were really good. I knew when we saw old Bike Boy at the Battle of the Bands that he had star quality. It's funny, he was so serious and melodramatic when he was performing on stage that time, but he's very cheerful and friendly in real life. Some of the other cast members looked a bit awkward sometimes when they were walking around the stage, but he and John Kowalski (for that is the name of the mysterious boy) looked totally comfortable, like there was nothing weird about standing up in front of a bunch of girls they didn't know and walking about reading lines. Susie Murray was very good too. You'd never know from just talking to her about made-up youth hostels and train directions in German that she was such a good actress. I suppose those conversations didn't really show her acting range.

Of course, I did not join the musical to just stand there while Vanessa strutted about the stage like she was at her stupid birthday party, so after a while I did start to feel a bit annoyed. But then Cathy reminded us chorus people that we weren't just a little choir, we were actors too, so we had to remember this when we were on stage. In some scenes we had to be other nannies; in others we'd be at the races and in others we'd be dressed as servants. Then she took the lead actors aside and us lowly chorus folk started to run through some songs with Ms Byrne.

Ms Byrne said she hoped we'd been listening to our soundtrack CDs over the weekend (I had, as you know). Then she told us she was going to change some of the songs that are just sung by one or two characters in the film. *Mary Poppins* is not a musical with big chorus numbers – most of the songs are just sung by one character. But now the chorus are going to join in for parts of those songs (I tried not to think that this means that basically we will be Vanessa's backing singers).

We started going through the chorus of 'Feed the Birds' and after a while it actually sounded quite good. And to make it even better, Alice and I started acting out the words to each other very enthusiastically. Ms Byrne noticed and told us to 'stop messing', which is very unfair because Cathy had just told us we were meant to acting when we were singing. How can you get into trouble for doing what you're told? Truly this world is very unfair. Alice said this very politely and Ms Byrne said that for the moment she just wanted us to learn the songs and 'not think about acting until you can actually sing' which wasn't very nice. I think she should be trying harder to encourage our creativity.

But still, it was all much more fun than what I'd normally have been doing on a Monday afternoon, ie trying to avoid my mother giving me some sort of lecture, which is basically how I spend my time at home. It all went on longer than we expected, so when it was over Alice had to rush off to get her lift and she didn't get to say anything to Bike Boy. He did give her a cheerful wave when she was leaving, though, which was good, I think. I was looking for Cass when Karen smirked at me.

'I hope you're ready to watch everything I do,' she said. 'Seeing as you're my understudy. If anything happens to me, you're going to have to be able to recreate my performance. Perfectly.'

I tried to think of something clever to say to that but I couldn't. So I just said, 'Well, I bet that won't be hard.'

Karen gave this ridiculous affected laugh. So much for her getting a bit better since the Battle of the Bands. It looks like this musical, combined with her fairytale prince Bernard, has gone to her head. Which is all I need.

'It's okay if you're jealous,' she said. 'I know it's hard for you to be out of the spotlight, after your wonderful show at the Battle of the Bands.'

'It's fine, actually,' I said.

Karen ignored me. 'If you need any advice on acting or singing, I'd be glad to help,' she said. 'Bernard – that's my boy-friend, by the way, he goes to the Mary Ann Norland Drama School – says he thinks I'm a natural actress.'

'Maybe he was practising his own acting when he said it,' said Cass, who had emerged from the backstage group. 'Come on, Bex.'

And off we went.

'God, I can't believe I have to be her understudy,' I said. 'It's like Ms Byrne is just tormenting me.'

'Well, she doesn't know how awful Karen is,' said Cass, which is true, I suppose. 'So,' Cass went on, 'how was the rehearsal? Apart from Karen, obviously.'

So I told her, and asked what they'd been up to backstage. She said it was brilliant. They all sat in a circle and came up with set and prop ideas. Everyone was really into it. Cass was a bit disappointed because Ms Doyle said some of her ideas were 'a bit ambitious' (apparently they can't move the whole set up and down to make it look like Mary Poppins is flying, which was Cass's favourite idea), but she liked some of the others so they're all going to start doing sketches soon. Ellie was disappointed because the famous Mrs Limond wasn't there. Instead, she just had to make lists of all the cast members with Ms Doyle and figure out how many different costumes were needed for all the different scenes.

'But she says it all feels very, y'know, theatrical,' said Cass.

And I know what she means. Even during the slightly boring bits, there's something exciting about it all, knowing we're all coming together to put on a giant spectacular show. It must really be my theatrical blood coming out at last. Maybe this is all the beginning of a glamorous career and in twenty years I'll be on the *Late Late Show* saying, 'Yes, it all began when I was in the chorus of *Mary Poppins*. One of the leading actors became terribly ill on the opening night and I, as the understudy, had to take over while she was being very, very sick backstage. My performance as Michael was hailed by the critics as one of the greatest stage debuts of all time.'

It could happen, anyway.

TUESDAY ☾

The class has gone musical mad. I am starting to feel a bit bad for Emma because we were all talking about the rehearsal at lunch and she's the only one of our gang who isn't in it. Not that she seems to mind, hugely. She's started doing these new after-school computer classes and by the time the musical's over she wants to have created some sort of artificial intelligence.

'It's only a matter of time before computers can think for themselves,' she said, which sounds a bit scary to me, but Emma seems quite excited about it.

Anyway, everyone who's taking part is all giddy about the musical. I think some of the teachers are getting annoyed because we're so distracted. Miss Kelly said that musicals were all very well, but how much energy would the whole thing consume, and would *Mary Poppins* seem important in a few years when we were all fighting over water and batteries in the streets? Mrs Harrington, on the other hand, was very enthusiastic, which somehow was even more annoying. She asked who was playing what, and when she found out Vanessa and Karen had big parts she was thrilled. She loves Karen because when she kept going on about my mum's book last term, Karen egged her on (just to annoy me, of course).

Then she turned to me.

'And what about you, Rebecca?' she said. 'If your mammy's wonderful book told me anything, it's that you know all about showbiz!'

And just when I thought she'd given up on that nonsense!

'Um,' I said. 'I'm in the chorus.'

Mrs Harrington's smile faltered for a moment.

'Well, that's very good too!' she said brightly. 'I'm sure your mammy is very proud!'

I didn't say anything. I just glowered. Mrs Harrington obviously gave up on me then because she went back to talking about some boring poem or other.

But despite all this, Jessie, Ellie, Cass, Alice and I are full of excitement about the musical (and Emma seems a little bit excited on our behalf, though admittedly not as excited as she seems to be about computers developing minds of their own and taking over the world). Alice is especially full of excitement about Bike Boy, but she doesn't really want to talk about it to anyone apart from me and Cass. So it wasn't until school was over and we were getting our coats that she had a chance to say anything about it.

'He seemed quite friendly,' she said. 'Didn't he?'

'Definitely,' said Cass. 'He came over to us, remember?'

'And he waved to you at the end, even though you were rushing out,' I said.

'Oh God,' said Alice. 'I hope he doesn't think I was avoiding him. Do you think it might have looked like I was, y'know, running away?'

We assured her it didn't, but she didn't seem convinced. I don't think she'll be able to relax until she sees him again tomorrow and is able to show him that she doesn't want to, like, flee the room whenever he's around. I had forgotten how neurotic being in love can make someone. I bet I was never like this with Paperboy. I haven't mentioned him to anyone all week. But I have thought about him a bit.

LATER

Actually, now I come to think of it, I haven't thought about him half as much as I was doing a week or so ago. The musical really is a good distraction. Maybe I will not be a hollow shell of a girl forever after all?

WEDNESDAY ✿

Rehearsal day! I think we are getting quite good at our musical songs already. Alice and I are altos, which mean we sing slightly lower than the squeaky little sopranos. Because we are officially doing the low parts sometimes I keep singing in a sort of fake-booming voice for a laugh which does not amuse Ms Byrne and will not bode well for me once she figures out where exactly in the chorus it's coming from. I don't know what it is about these rehearsals; they are bringing out my high spirits. Which is a good thing, I think, after all these months of terrible misery.

Anyway, we are coming along quite well, even though it's only the second rehearsal. Of course, the only downside is having to endure Karen Rodgers and Vanessa prancing about the place. They were doing more of that stagecraft business and something called 'blocking', which means figuring out who is meant to be where on stage, and we had to be a chorus behind them. For 'Feed the Birds', we're meant to be people just walking about the streets, and when Mary Poppins starts singing about this old lady selling bird seed we all stop what we're doing and join in. Today we didn't actually do any singing; we just practised parading about and stopping at the right time.

It would have been quite fun really – it felt like proper putting-on-a-show stuff – if the people standing in front of us hadn't included Karen and Vanessa. I can't tell which of them's worse. They keep asking Cathy ridiculous questions really seriously like they're proper actors and she's Steven Spielberg or someone. For some freakish reason she doesn't seem to mind; in fact she seems to like it! I have to admit, I am losing all respect for her. They even STAND in an annoying way. I didn't even think that was possible, but it turns out it is.

Alice didn't mind all this of course because she was gazing at Bike Boy. I don't think she was the only one, but I didn't tell her that. Lots of people were gawping at him and his mysterious friend John Kowalski as they are the only boys with proper parts (there is another boy called Sam playing Uncle Albert but he's only in it for one scene and he spends most of his time helping out the backstage boys who are learning about sets and lights with Cass and co). It's not really surprising that we were distracted by their presence – after all, we do go to an all-girls school. I have to admit I looked at them a bit myself. But I think it's because I'm trying to figure out whether John Kowalski is good-looking or not. It's weirdly hard to tell. Quite the opposite of Paperboy. Not that I want to think about *him*, as he still hasn't mailed me.

Anyway, Alice is much happier now because when the boys were walking out at the end of the rehearsal Bike Boy stopped and asked how she was getting on in the chorus. Alice barely had time to say, 'It's fun, thanks' when one of the boys – I think it was that sulky John – called, 'Come on, Ritch,' and Bike Boy said, 'Sorry, I'd better go – see you on Friday.' Which, as I said to Alice, shows that he does not think she is a crazy person and he doesn't want to avoid her. So she is in a very good mood.

FRIDAY :)

School is even more boring than usual now we have the rehearsals to look forward to. It's like time goes by even more slowly when we're dying to get to the next rehearsal. Which was great fun this afternoon. To be honest, if I'd known this musical would be such a laugh, I'd have signed up anyway, even if I hadn't wanted to bond with Cass and Alice again and if Alice hadn't hurt her wrist.

And, luckily, we didn't have anything to do with the main actors today so I didn't have to endure watching Vanessa and Karen parading about like they're Kate Winslet and Gwyneth Paltrow. We were just singing our chorus songs AND Ms Byrne said it was okay for us to do a bit of singing-acting so Alice and I got to make excellent sad faces when we sang about the poor old bird woman in 'Feed The Birds'. Alice's was very good, you'd really think she was feeling miserable, which she definitely isn't.

Also, because I am a very noble friend now, I am genuinely thrilled for Alice about the magical return of Bike Boy. It adds a bit of extra drama to the whole thing. Because he was doing the lead actor practice today and we were at the other end of the hall singing around a piano, we didn't come into contact with him that often during the actual rehearsal, but when it was over Alice and I had put our coats on and were drinking cartons of juice while we waited for Cass (we need to keep our energy up, all that singing is very tiring) when Bike Boy came over with the mysterious John Kowalski.

'Hey,' said Bike Boy, smiling at us (but mostly, I think, at Alice). 'This is John.'

John Kowalski nodded towards us and said, 'Hello.'

'So,' said Bike Boy, or Richard as I should really call him. 'How was your rehearsal?'

I was going to say something, but then I realised that if I want to be a good friend I should let Alice talk. So I did. John Kowalski didn't say anything either; he just stood there looking all amused and aloof, as usual. I have to admit he's quite intriguing. In fact, I was so busy wondering what he was thinking I didn't really listen to Alice and Bike Boy until Bike Boy said, 'So, are you heading out now?'

Alice was starting to say 'Actually, we're waiting for ...' when Cass emerged from behind the scenes (or rather all the ropes and curtains and old props at the side of the stage) with her coat on and headed over to join us. So Alice said, 'Oh, here she is! Yes, we're going now.'

Richard and John Kowalski had their backs to both me and Cass as she approached us, so she was able to make a 'Oooh, look at this!' face at me and I was able to make one back at her. When she reached us Richard introduced her to John, who just said, 'Hi,' in his lofty way, and we all walked out of the school together. Cass and I let Richard and Alice do most of the talking. I felt a bit awkward about John Kowalski, but he didn't seem to care about talking to us. It wasn't like he was ignoring us. He just seemed ... self-contained. Just strolling along.

Richard collected his famous bike (which was chained to a lamp post on the school drive), and when we got to the gate we all stood there not saying anything. John Kowalski clearly doesn't do small talk.

'See you tomorrow, Richard?' he said.

'Yeah, see you then,' said Bike Boy.

John Kowalski turned to me, Cass and Alice.

'Ladies,' he said. Then he smiled properly for the first time, which completely changed his face and made him look much nicer, raised his right hand to his brow in a sort of joking salute, and turned on his heel and strode off down Griffith Avenue, his big khaki wool overcoat whirling behind him.

Heavens.

Anyway, Cass and I said we'd better go too (so Alice could have a few moments alone with her true love) so we said bye to her and Bike Boy and went down the road in the same direction as John Kowalski. We crossed to the other side in case there was an awkward catching-up moment, but actually he walks so fast that he was way too far ahead of us to catch. He is a mysterious fellow.

Anyway, Cass and I had a good chat on the way down the road. She asked if I'd heard from Paperboy, and I had to say I hadn't, and she said not to worry because he was probably just overwhelmed by the wild landscape of Canada.

'Maybe he's got lost in a forest, or something?' she said.

I knew she was trying to cheer me so I didn't remind her that I do know he's in Vancouver and is unlikely to have got lost in any wilderness (unless that school trip went horribly wrong. Surely not).

SATURDAY ☺

I didn't even bother trying to have a lie-in today. I knew my mother would come in and drag me out of bed so I just got up early. Of course, when I came downstairs at an ungodly hour (half nine) my parents stared at me and pretended to be shocked.

'Look, Rosie, she's awake!' said my dad. He is so not funny even though he thinks he's hilarious.

Anyway, it was quite a good thing that I was up early because Jane sent me a text asking about Alice and saying she'd be in town later if we happened to be around. As it happened, Cass and I had been talking about the possibility of going in to try on make-up testers (Rachel says this is a bad idea because all those tester products are full of germs but we've never caught anything off them. Yet.) so we decided to meet up in the Pepperpot Café, which sells the most beautiful hot chocolate in the world (it is not cheap, though, so sometimes Cass and I just share one).

'So,' said Jane. 'Has Vanessa changed her ways?'

Cass and I just looked at each other.

'No,' I said. 'In fact, she's almost worse than ever.'

Jane sighed. 'I was afraid this might happen,' she said. 'Her mum was in our house the other day and said that they were really impressed by how hard she was working at the musical and they think she's really learned a lesson from the party. So they've been lavishing her with praise to encourage her.'

'Oh my God, like she needs any encouragement,' said Cass, gloomily.

'It's alright for you, Cass,' I said. 'You're back stage designing, I dunno, merry-go-rounds and chimney pots and things. I'm the one who has to look at her!'

'Well, I can hear her,' said Cass. 'All the lead actors practise down our end of the hall, so I can't avoid it. She keeps saying things like "I can't really understand my motivation in this scene, Cathy, can you help me?'"

We all felt quite gloomy at the thought of Vanessa. But the hot chocolate helped us cheer up a bit and we spent ages just talking nonsense about telly programmes and our equally hideous schools (Jane was quite impressed by Miss Kelly, she says her geography teacher is much more boring). It was a fun afternoon really. And a few weeks ago I never thought I'd write those words again. I think my life might actually be getting better.

MONDAY

I knew this would happen. Being *Mary Poppins* has completely gone to Vanessa's head. It was only a matter of time. And we should have known that if the whole party humiliation didn't dent her confidence than nothing would. She was bad enough in the rehearsals last week, but today she went TOO FAR. And I bet it won't stop here.

The rehearsal was going on as usual – the lead parts were working on some scenes, we were at the other end working on songs, and then we came together towards the end. We were practising our stopping and starting and Cathy was going through each actor's parts so there were times when Vanessa had nothing to do. This meant she was just standing there on the 'stage'. Or at least, she was meant to. Instead she walked over to us in the chorus and said, 'Hey, can I get a chair over here?'

Like she was a film star and we were her minions! Of course, we all just stared at her. Which of course made her even worse.

'Come on,' she said, and gave a horrible little laugh. 'Go and get me a chair, someone. It's not like you lot have got anything better to do.' A few of the chorus laughed or snorted with rage, but no one dared say anything out loud because Cathy and Ms Byrne would have noticed.

Then a voice came from the other side of the stage.

'If you really have lost the use of your legs,' it drawled, 'I suppose you can take my seat.'

It was John Kowalski, who wasn't in this scene either and had been sitting to the side of the rehearsal area. He got up and handed Vanessa his chair.

'Ooh, thanks!' said Vanessa. I swear she batted her eyelashes at him. I didn't think anyone actually did that in real life.

But John Kowalski didn't say anything, he just raised his

eyebrows and went back to the side of the space, where he leaned against the wall and folded his arms. He really is very tall.

Vanessa looked at the rest of us in a smug way and said, 'At least someone has some consideration for what us real actors are going through!'

And I swear I saw John Kowalski roll his eyes. He didn't look like he'd given away his chair because he liked Vanessa or thought she needed a seat. He looked like he'd done it to shut her up.

She didn't seem to think this, though. She looked even more smug than ever as she sat down on her new throne. She's probably missing having Caroline around to do her bidding. I actually feel sorry for Caroline; she must be feeling very left out of all this musical stuff. I think she and Alison should team up and leave Karen and Vanessa to each other. I mean, I'm not hugely fond of either Caroline or Alison, but I don't dislike them. They deserve better than their bossy pals.

Bike Boy and Alice had another little chat at the end of the rehearsal so Cass and I left them to it. I have to admit that I do feel a little bit jealous of Alice because my own love life is such a misery and a sham (still no mail, of course). But I am trying my absolute best to stick to my life rules and be happy for her. I feel very noble.

TUESDAY ☾

I am starting to wish my parents hadn't been in that musical after all. They keep going on about it. I'm almost scared to mention rehearsals because the word 'musical' and indeed 'rehearsal' sends them off on a terrifying trip down memory lane. Tonight Mum finally found the photos of their performance and I have never seen anything like it in my life.

'I thought *The Pirates of Penzance* was set in Victorian times!' I said. 'What on earth are you wearing?'

'Oh, we thought we'd bring it up to date a bit,' said Mum. 'A sort of post-punk, New Wave, New Romantic thing.'

I have no idea what any of that means, but the results were terrifying.

'Why is your hair like that?' I said.

'It's just back-combing,' she said. 'And a LOT of hairspray. Quite a scary amount really'

'You nearly went on fire when that girl Fiona lit a cigarette backstage,' said Dad.

But his 'look' for the musical wasn't much better.

'What are you wearing there?' I said. 'I thought you were meant to be a pirate! Pirates don't wear golden harem pants and ... is that a purple blouse?'

'It was the fashion!' said Dad quite defensively. 'Everyone thought I was very cool, I'll have you know.'

I bet they didn't.

'It was fun!' said Mum.

It's made me count my blessings, anyway. As far as I know we're going to have fairly ordinary costumes. The famous Mrs Limond is meant to be coming in soon and Ellie is very excited. All she's got to do so far is measure members of the cast and make lists. But this week she should actually get to make something. She's been practising on her mum's sewing machine and everything, though she couldn't practise for long last night because her mum wanted to make some new robes for their Spring Goddess Renewal ceremony which is coming up soon.

WEDNESDAY

Miss Kelly isn't the only teacher who's getting fed up with the musical. Mrs O'Reilly was pretty annoyed today too.

'I can always tell when it's one of your rehearsal days,' she said crossly. 'Half the class are even more distracted than usual. Don't you want to do well in your Junior Cert?'

'But Mrs O'Reilly,' said Vanessa loudly. 'We're learning lots of important skills in the musical. It's part of a well-rounded education.'

We all froze. No one talks back to Mrs O'Reilly. Ever. Even the cheekiest girls. When she gives out to you, you just have to sit there and take it.

'Miss Finn,' said Mrs O'Reilly, dryly. 'You may be the star of the musical, but in my classroom you are a student of history. And that's the part of your well-rounded education I want you to concentrate on today. If you disagree, I'm sure we can arrange a trip to the principal's office and we can see what she thinks your priority should be.'

I have to admit I was torn. A part of me actually agreed with Vanessa (for the first time ever), but then again, it was Vanessa. It is very hard for me to feel as though I am on her side. Anyway, even she's not stupid enough to push Mrs O'Reilly so she said sorry in a surprisingly humble voice and shut up.

She didn't stay humble for long, though. At rehearsal, it appeared that she really has decided that John Kowalski is her new victim! She kept sort of sidling up to him and chatting at him. I am pleased to say that he didn't seem to be very impressed. In fact, at one stage she said something to him and he just went 'Really? How fascinating,' and walked off. I have to admit that I was glad to see this. Not, of course, that I care about John Kowalski. But it's nice to see Vanessa not getting just what she wants for once.

Sadly this didn't seem to deter her. When we were getting our coats to go home she said, 'That John guy is so into me, it's getting embarrassing.'

I have no idea why she was talking to me, by the way. The only time she's ever paid me any attention was when she wanted to use me to get on that stupid telly programme. But as Caroline isn't at rehearsals, I suppose anyone will do when she feels like having a bit of a boast.

Anyway, I didn't say anything because I didn't want to encourage her, but I had forgotten that Vanessa doesn't really notice other people.

'He can't take his eyes off me,' she said. 'And he told me I was fascinating earlier. I suppose it's flattering, really. Like, he's not totally hideous or anything.'

It's lucky I had decided I wasn't going to say anything to her because really, what could I say to that? Apart from 'HE WAS BEING SARCASTIC' which he clearly was. Wasn't he? Anyway, she had her coat on by that stage, so she strutted off. I am surprised by how annoyed I was. I didn't think it was possible for Vanessa to irritate me even more, but I actually wanted to kick her.

THURSDAY

Just realised I have barely thought about Paperboy all week. It must be the magic of show business. Speaking of which, my parents are still going on about their mental musical. This evening at dinner (for which I had had to chop two onions even though they made my eyes water) they started waffling on to me and Rachel about how Mum flew over the stage in a harness. I can't tell Cass that; she's obsessed with trying to get Mary Poppins to fly, even though Ms Doyle keeps telling her the school can't afford the insurance.

Apparently, things were a bit more free and easy back in the '80s. Mum had dug out a picture of her singing while basically dangling from a rope. Her giant mane looked even bigger from that angle.

'Weren't you scared?' said Rachel. 'It doesn't look very safe.'

'Oh, it was grand,' said Mum.

'Apart from that night you got stuck up there for half an hour,' said Dad.

'That was fine too,' said Mum, stiffly. 'We just improvised a bit so it was like the Pirate King was, you know, there in spirit during the next few scenes. Hovering over the action.'

'Oh yeah,' said Dad. 'And then when they finally got you down, you sort of tumbled into the policemen and said 'Arrrrrr!' like a real pirate. And then you danced off the stage and came back for the Pirate King's next scene. You were very good.'

I can't imagine we'd be able to improvise if Vanessa was suspended from a rope for half an hour (I, of course, would be too busy laughing with evil glee). We're all only just about getting the hang of moving and singing at the same time. Apart from Vanessa, annoyingly enough. I wish she wasn't so good. And John Kowalski too, of course.

Speaking of him, I find it hard to believe, but it looks like he might return Vanessa's crazed affections. She had him basically backed into a corner during the rehearsal break today. Cass, Alice and I were talking to Bike Boy (who makes a beeline towards Alice whenever he can), and when he noticed Vanessa and John talking (or rather, Vanessa talking at John) he said, 'God, it looks like Kowalski's found himself a new girlfriend. About time too, it's been ages since he broke up with his last one.'

I know it's got nothing to do with me, but I am very disappointed he likes Vanessa! He doesn't look that shallow. Or deaf.

LATER

Or blind.

FRIDAY ☺

I just spent ages at the corner of Griffith Avenue talking to John Kowalski. Hmmm. I feel a bit funny about it. Not sure what I think. I am going to go to bed now.

SATURDAY ☺

Sooo ... yesterday was a bit strange.

First of all, I must make it clear that I do not fancy John Kowalski. My heart belongs to Paperboy, even though he hasn't mailed me for weeks. But I still feel weirdly guilty. Which is ridiculous because I bet Paperboy is talking to girls all the time. I mean, I'd be talking to boys regularly (I presume) if I went to a mixed school.

Anyway, this is what happened. Today's rehearsal was only an hour long (Cass says this is because the teachers all want to escape to the pub and that's why they end some Friday rehearsals earlier), so we didn't get a break, but at the end Bike Boy came over to Alice and started chatting to her. And I felt like a bit of a gooseberry so I went off to find Cass. She was up on the stage, putting away some tools.

'This whole set designing thing involves an awful lot of hacking up cardboard,' she said when I came up. 'My hands are killing me. I'm much more feeble than I thought. Where's Alice?'

'Look!' I said, and gestured in a very subtle way at the other end of the hall, where Alice and Bike Boy were deep in conversation.

‘Oooh,’ said Cass.

‘What should we do?’ I said. ‘I mean, I don’t want to interrupt them. But I don’t want to just sneak out without saying goodbye.’

‘Hmm,’ said Cass. ‘I think sneaking might be the best option. I mean, you’re doing it out of niceness. She’ll understand why.’

‘But what if she looks for us and we’ve vanished?’ I said. ‘Then Bike Boy will think she’s been abandoned by her mates. That won’t look very good.’

So we decided we’d walk out and call ‘Bye!’ to her as we went. Then she could decide whether to come out with us or not. And as it turned out, she didn’t. She just waved and smiled at us, so we left her to it.

‘She can’t stay that long,’ I said as trudged up the school drive. ‘Her dad will be out to give her a lift in ten minutes.’

‘Oh well, at least she’ll spend those ten minutes with Bike Boy,’ said Cass.

I said goodbye to Cass when we got to the gate; she wasn’t walking down with me to her estate as usual because she was meeting Liz in town for hot chocolate. I try not to be jealous when she goes to meet Liz, but I am a bit. It’s not like I mind my friends having other friends – I mean, Alice and I became best friends when we were tiny and that didn't change when we became friends with Cass when we started secondary school. And we're all friendly with Ellie and Emma and Jessie. But this is the first time any of us have had a really good friend who isn't friends with the others. It makes me feel a bit weird.

Not that it's the only thing that makes me feel weird at the moment. After I said goodbye to Cass, I reached into my bag to get my iPod. And maybe it was because it was freezing cold and my fingers weren't working properly, but as soon as I got it out of my bag, I dropped it in a pile of leaves. I was rummaging around in the leaves when I noticed a pair of large-ish leather boots attached to a pair of long school-trousered legs next to me, and then a tall boy bent down, reached into the leaves, and pulled out my iPod by the earphones.

'Is this what you were looking for?' said John Kowalski because, of course, that is who it was. None of the other boys around here would wear those cool, battered kind of old-fashioned boots. Well, actually, Bike Boy would totally wear them. But as far as I can tell the other boys in the musical all wear giant runners.

'Oh,' I said. 'Yeah. Thanks.' He had a book in his hand,

another well-worn paperback. But a very familiar one because it was *On the Road* and my parents have the exact same edition. Which is probably why, without really thinking, I said, 'Oh, is your book any good? My parents have that edition of it.'

He looked a bit surprised, and said, 'It's fantastic. You haven't read it, then?'

And I had to say no. I felt weirdly disappointed I couldn't tell him I had and then talk to him about it.

So anyway, he said, 'Oh, you should. It'll show you how pointless it is to live by society's stupid conventions.'

There isn't really much you can say to that, at least if you haven't read the book, so I said, 'Oh, really?' And then felt very stupid. I felt I had to say something intelligent to show that, actually, I do read proper books (which I do). But, for some reason, the only book I could think of was Gerald Durrell's *My Family and Other Animals*, which is an excellent book but is also not very serious. And John Kowalski seems to like quite serious things. But anyway, I found myself saying, 'I'm reading Gerald Durrell at the moment myself.'

And, to my surprise, John Kowalski said, 'You mean Laurence Durrell?'

I knew that was Gerald's annoying older brother Larry, who went on to become a famous author. I kind of wished I had been reading him instead because it sounded much more impressive. But I couldn't lie, so I told him that actually I was reading Laurence's brother Gerald.

'He wrote about animals and the wonders of nature,' I said grandly (I didn't mention that these wonders included his two puppies called Widdle and Puke. That didn't sound serious enough.).

John Kowalski didn't seem to mind that I wasn't reading Larry's books. He got quite intense and told me he was reading a lot of Walt Whitman at the moment. And then he stopped and said, 'Which way are you walking?'

I pointed down the road and said, 'That way.'

'Oh,' he said, and smiled his crooked smile. 'So am I.'

And so I found myself walking down Griffith Avenue with John Kowalski. I asked him why he was doing the musical (he really doesn't seem like a very musical type of person), and he told me he wants to write for the theatre and star in his own productions. So basically he needs theatrical experience and this is the nearest he can get to being in a play. 'It's still got the rawness of theatre,' he said. 'You're a prisoner of the spotlight.

There's no escape when you're on stage. And no place to hide.' (Actually, I suppose that isn't quite true. I mean, you could run off stage if you really wanted to. Or hide behind a prop or something).

Also, he said quite modestly, he can play the piano and sing a bit (apparently he sometimes plays keyboards in Richard's band). So doing the musical seemed like a good idea. Oh, and I am pretty sure he is NOT interested in Vanessa. When her name came up, he sort of shuddered and said, 'Oh God, her. She's driving me mad. Has she always been so crazy?' so I am able to respect him. Which would not have been possible if he'd liked Vanessa, even as a friend.

Anyway, I told him that I was in a band too and he looked quite impressed, and then I said that we were on hiatus because of Alice's wrist so we were doing the musical instead. And he asked if we wrote our own songs and I said we did, and told him how we all collaborate on all the different bits from the chords to the lyrics.

'So you're an artist,' he said.

'Well,' I said. 'Sort of.'

He looked at me.

'Never be ashamed to say you're an artist,' he said. And he

looked quite noble and dashing with his school scarf flung over his shoulder like he was about to go into battle.

'Oh,' I said. 'I won't.' We had reached the corner where I turn off the avenue and I said, 'Um, I live up there.'

'Oh, right,' said John Kowalski. 'I live down there.' But he didn't move. Instead, he got out a packet of cigarettes and lit one. I wanted to say that I didn't like smoking, but he started telling me that he's writing a novel about a young man who goes off to fight in the Spanish Civil War in the 1930s and becomes a bullfighter.

'It's about believing in a glorious ideal,' he said passionately, waving his cigarette around. 'About losing all physical fear.'

It sounds very dramatic. And I could probably do with losing some physical fear myself. I'm quite a coward really. Alice sometimes goes horse riding near her house and I've always been too scared to go because it is surprising how high up you are when you're on a horse and they also have giant heads that are very hard to control with the reins.

I told him that my mum writes novels (I didn't mention Ruthie O'Reilly, of course), but when I said she was Rosie Carberry he said that he didn't read 'crude mainstream best-sellers'. I was about to defend Mum's books (God knows why,

I think they're pretty awful), but then he asked if I wrote anything. And even though I've only ever talked about this with Alice, I found myself telling him that I did write stories when I was younger, but I've got out of the habit of it now.

'But if it's in your blood,' said John very intensely. He says a lot of things very intensely. 'You owe it to yourself to write again. Maybe you even owe it to the world!'

Maybe he's right. Maybe I am really destined to be a great writer. If I'm being honest with myself, I have to admit that this is quite unlikely, but when he was talking I wanted it to be true. I was going to tell him that I do write a diary and I might even have told him about the poems but before I could say anything my phone rang. And I had to answer it because it was Mum, who was ranting on about how late I was and how she was worried sick and how I had to come home this instant. So when I hung up I turned to John Kowalski and said, 'That was my mother. She's not writing at the moment. She's yelling at me to come home.'

'Ah,' said John Kowalski. 'I should probably be at home now too. I'll see you at rehearsal.'

And no sooner had I said goodbye than he stamped out his cigarette and off he went down Gracepark Road into the murky evening, his scarf flowing out behind him like a banner. He was wearing his cool woollen khaki coat that sort of swept about. There's something very dramatic about John Kowalski himself. It's not surprising he writes about wars and bullfighters and stuff.

So I walked up in the other direction, feeling a bit funny. I rang Alice later to tell her what happened. She was very cheerful after her conversation with Bike Boy.

'He's so nice!' she burbled. 'He was saying what a shame it was that Hey Dollface were on hiatus because he thought I was a really good guitarist.'

'Wow,' I said. 'Well, he's right.'

'But I couldn't stay talking to him for too long because of my lift. Thanks for, you know, leaving me to it.'

'Well, we didn't want to disturb you,' I said. 'I do care about your feelings, Alice.' I paused. 'Um, I got talking to someone too.'

'What?' said Alice. 'Who?'

'You know John Kowalski who's playing Mr Banks?'

'Of course,' said Alice.

'Well, I got talking to him at the gates and walked down to Gracepark Road with him,' I said. 'And we were talking for a good bit.'

'Oh, right,' said Alice. 'Is he nice?'

Is he nice? I'm not actually sure. I mean, he's not NOT nice. But he's not all cheerful and friendly like, well, like Paperboy.

'He's very interesting,' I said. 'But ... I feel a bit guilty. About Paperboy.'

There was silence on the other end of the line. Then Alice said, 'Well, you know, Bex, you've got nothing to feel guilty about.'

'I know,' I said. 'But ...'

'You just talked to another boy for a few minutes! Even if Paperboy was actually in Dublin, you shouldn't have to feel guilty about that!'

'True,' I said. 'But ...'

'And besides,' said Alice, who was getting quite worked up (obviously talking to Bike Boy had over-stimulated her), 'you have to embrace life, Bex! You can't put everything on hold just because Paperboy went to Canada!' She sounded a bit like John Kowalski. Everyone seems to be into embracing life this weekend.

I know she is right and I told her so and she said, 'So you don't feel guilty?' And I said I didn't, even though I do a bit. And she said, 'I just don't want you to, I dunno, spend all your time thinking about Paperboy and not actually, like, noticing what's happening around you.'

Which is, I think, though I didn't say it, an Alice-ish way of saying she doesn't think me and Paperboy are going out anymore.

Everyone wants to convince me that me and Paperboy have split up. And I have to admit that I understand why. But still. I don't like it. If it was official we weren't really going out anymore, it would make me too sad. And it would also make me hate Paperboy as it would mean that he had dumped me without even bothering to tell me, which is a terrible thing to do. And I can't believe he's that bad.

Is he?

SUNDAY ☼

Oh my God! I got a mail from Paperboy at last! And it looks like he hasn't dumped me without telling me. I hope. I mean, he didn't say, 'Oh, Rebecca, I will love you forever.' But then he didn't say he didn't. It was actually a very normal mail. He apologised for not mailing me sooner and said that everything had been mad at his new school with the trip away and everything and he'd actually forgotten it was his turn to mail me. He thought I was going to mail him and then he eventually checked and realised it was his turn. And then he told me about his school trip and how he'd got really into snowboarding. That was about it, really.

When I read it I felt very relieved that he still signed his mail with some Xs. And I feel bad about thinking he would dump me without telling me. But I can't help thinking he shouldn't have forgotten it was his turn to mail me. And it took him weeks to even check! To be honest, I feel kind of annoyed with him now. I'm certainly not going to mail him back straight away. I'll make him wait and see how he likes that.

Of course, I had to read his mail really quickly. My mother hovered over me practically the whole time, as she always does. She and Dad have a computer each, but she refuses to get me and Rebecca a computer even to share. She says it's 'a ridiculous extravagance', and she doesn't approve of teenagers having constant access to the internet. So, instead, I'm only allowed go online on her or Dad's computer for about two seconds at a time. It's like the middle ages around here.

Anyway, after I got the mail, I rang Alice. I didn't actually say, 'Look, I told you we hadn't broken up!' but I almost did.

I thought Alice would be pleased for me, and she sort of was, but then she said, 'Hang on, do you mean you haven't had a mail from him at all since that one where he said he was going on the school trip? That was weeks ago!'

'I know,' I said.

'Oh,' said Alice.

'And I didn't tell you because I was trying to stick to my rule and not bother you with my troubles,' I said, nobly.

'Oh Bex,' said Alice. 'I don't want you to think you can't, like, tell me stuff.'

Well, really. This was very nice of her and everything, but one minute I'm too selfish and just thinking of my own problems, and the next I'm bottling everything up! I really can't win. I just had a bash on the sofa with my drum sticks to release my frustrations, but the sofa is just not the same as my drums.

MONDAY

Felt a bit odd seeing John Kowalski after our big talk on Friday. I mean, are we friends now? I have to admit I was a bit worried he'd act like nothing had happened, but he didn't. He and

Bike Boy arrived at the rehearsal at the last minute and then he was off practising with the leads so I didn't really come into contact with him until we were all going home. He was on his way out of the hall, wearing that weird yet strangely cool old coat, but when he saw me he paused.

'Hello, Miss Rafferty,' he said. 'Did you write anything over the weekend, then?'

The only thing I'd written over the weekend were big diary entries, partly about him, so I said, 'Well, no, not really.'

'Ah well,' he said airily. 'It's only a matter of time. Go and write something brilliant. See you.'

And off he went.

I really do not know what I think of him at all.

Cass, of course, is sure she knows what I think of him. She was watching us from her prop den on the stage, and when he walked off she jumped off the stage and ran over to me.

'Oh my God,' she said. 'He fancies you. And I think you fancy him back.'

'I do not!' I said. I have a horrible feeling I went bright red. 'He smokes!'

'Hmmm,' said Cass. 'I think you do. I don't think you care about his smoking.'

'Oh, shut up, Cass,' I said, but not in a mean way. I hope. Cass didn't seem to take offence anyway because she laughed and said, 'Well, I don't blame you if you do. He's not bad-looking really. Though he's not my type.'

'I don't fancy anyone,' I said. 'Apart from Paperboy.'

But if I'm being very honest, I am not entirely sure if this is true.

TUESDAY ☾

I keep thinking about John Kowalski. There was something about the way he called me 'Miss Rafferty' that made me feel a bit funny. But how can I feel anything at all about him when Paperboy is my true love? Also, he is not as good-looking as Paperboy (even when he smiles, although I have to admit that he looks pretty good when he does that). He is also much more intense and serious than Paperboy. Whenever we talked about what we wanted to do when we grew up Paperboy was always a bit vague and said he'd thought about being either a designer or a doctor but he wasn't quite sure. But John Kowalski seems totally sure about his future as some sort of writing/acting genius. It is a bit intimidating, really.

But also quite interesting.

WEDNESDAY ✿

Got into trouble at rehearsal today and it was all Cass's fault. The chorus were practising in the main part of the hall, and Alice and I were at the edge of the group. Which meant we could see the side of the stage where Cass was doing mysterious set stuff, but Ms Byrne, whose back was to the stage, couldn't.

Anyway, we were singing away ('Supercalifragilisticexpialidocious', as it happens) and then I noticed Cass's head rising slowly from behind a wooden car left over from last year's production of *Grease*. She made a hideous face at us and sank back down again. Alice and I both started laughing, but when Ms Byrne glanced over at us we cunningly disguised our sniggers by pretending to cough (I am very good at covering up laughter by coughing, sneezing and, in one instance, crying. You'd have to be if you sat next to Cass on a regular basis. Sometimes she lives to torment me, if by tormenting you mean 'make me laugh in class and get into trouble'.).

That was bad enough, but a few minutes later Cass did it

again, only this time she had a pair of giant sunglasses (probably left over from *Grease*) pushed up on her head. She looked upwards as if she didn't know how they had got there, and sank back down again. And a few minutes later she appeared slowly from behind an amplifier wearing a paper crown and a very serious expression before sinking behind it again.

It was too much for me and Alice. Even my best coughs couldn't hide our snickering. Basically, every time we calmed down, Cass would loom up behind a prop with something else ridiculous on her head, looking really solemn. By the time she appeared behind a lamp with a toy cactus on her head (where could it have come from?) Alice and I couldn't stop laughing. We didn't even bother to pretend to be sneezing or coughing and it wouldn't have made any difference if we had because I was laughing so much my shoulders were shaking. In the end Ms Byrne snapped at us and said that if we couldn't sing a simple song without sniggering like five-year-olds then we'd have to get out of the chorus and stop wasting her time. Cass must have heard this because she stopped looming up at us after that. So we calmed down again. I can't believe we nearly got ourselves kicked out of the musical because Cass had a cactus on her head!

It was pretty funny though.

I talked to John Kowalski for a few minutes during the break when I passed him on my way to the loo. He was coming from the direction of the door to the bike racks. I think he might have been having a smoke.

'So, Miss Rafferty,' he said. 'What was that Ms Byrne giving out to you chorus people about?'

'Ah,' I said. If it had been Paperboy, I would have told him all about Cass and he would have found it as funny as we did, but I had a feeling John Kowalski took things a bit more seriously. So I said, 'Someone from the backstage crew was trying to make us all laugh.'

'I hate that sort of messing about,' said John Kowalski vehemently. 'If you're working on a project, you have to give yourself to it, heart and soul.'

'Hmmm, I suppose so,' I said. 'Um, I'll see you later.' I suppose he is right, really. It wasn't as if it had disrupted the entire rehearsal or anything, but we were meant to be concentrating on singing.

Still, just thinking about Cass looming up behind that car makes me laugh. I am afraid I must be a very shallow person.

THURSDAY

It finally happened! Alice and Bike Boy are an item!

I only found out at school this morning because my stupid phone battery died yesterday evening without my noticing and SOMEONE (who might possibly be Rachel) was on the landline all night so Alice couldn't get through to me. Apparently, it happened last night when Alice was waiting for her lift. Her dad was a bit late and Bike Boy (or Richard as I really must call him now that he is Alice's boyfriend) kindly said he'd wait with her. And that's when it happened! Luckily they weren't still snogging when her dad finally turned up. Anyway, Bike Boy, I mean Richard, said he'd fancied her ever since the old days when we used to see him cycling down Calderwood Road and he thinks, and I quote, she's 'the coolest girl he's ever met'. Which is pretty good. Cass and I had to practically force her to tell us everything he said. She is never good at telling us when anyone has praised her.

Of course, Karen had to stick her oar in when Alice was telling us at the lockers this morning.

'Oh, so you and that Richard are seeing each other, are you?' she said. 'Even though you're both in the musical? I'd never mix business with pleasure. My boyfriend Bernard and I have sworn to always work on separate acting projects.'

Cass rolled her eyes. 'Yes, I'm sure you've both had loads of Hollywood offers. It must be so difficult choosing which ones to take.'

Karen literally tossed her head and put her hands on her hips. She has got much more theatrical since the musical started; it makes her worse than ever.

'It's an actor thing. You wouldn't understand,' she said. And she marched off with Alison by her side. Ugh, I hate her.

Everyone else who heard was happy for Alice, though. And I am too. Honestly. I am not really worried that she will abandon her old pals now she has a boyfriend and I only feel a tiny bit sad about my tragically lonely state.

I really am trying to stick to my rules. I haven't mailed Paperboy back, by the way. Let him wait. To be honest, I've got enough to think about right now without sending e-mails to someone who had to wait practically two months before they noticed they hadn't been in touch with me.

FRIDAY ☺

I think Caroline and Alison might really have formed an alliance. They had lunch together today while Vanessa and Karen paraded about near the whiteboard practising their lines and doing all our heads in. In days of yore the pair of them would have just sat there gazing in adoration at their heroines, but today they basically ignored them and kept chatting to each other. I hope they keep this up. They're quite nice really and, God knows, Karen and Vanessa deserve each other. And Emma says she's been getting on well with Alison at those computer classes. She is much nicer when she is away from Karen.

Something surprisingly exciting happened at rehearsal today – the arrival of Mrs Limond. We were all – chorus, main cast, backstage people – just pottering about doing our different things (Alice was trying hard not to gaze lovingly at Bike Boy) when the door opened with a crash and a very dramatic lady came in.

I guessed who she was straight away. She was about a hundred years old (okay, about seventy-five) but very tall and sort of regal. Her hair was a pale lavender colour and it was swept up in this amazing sort of poofy style. And she was wearing a very dramatic black floor-length coat with giant fluffy fur trimmings.

'Where is my cast?' she cried in an insanely posh, old-fashioned voice, the sort that practically sounds English.

'Mrs Limond!' said Cathy, running over to her. 'I'm Cathy Laverty, the director.'

Mrs Limond stared at her.

'You?' she said. 'But you're just a child!'

'Um, I'm twenty-five,' said Cathy. She sounded quite cross. 'I've got a degree in Drama. From Trinity.'

Mrs Limond waved a hand.

'That makes you a child in my eyes, girl. Now, where is my wardrobe assistant?'

Ellie put up her hand.

'Here,' she said, in a very small voice. 'My name's Ellie.'

'Aha!' said Mrs Limond. 'Come with me, Eleanor. Let's get to work. I hope you've got lots of measurements for me.' And with a click of her fingers, she swept out of the room. Ellie scurried after her. I bet she won't dare tell Mrs Limond her name isn't actually Eleanor; it's Galadriel. I don't think Mrs Limond is really the sort of person you can contradict.

Anyway, we were wondering where they'd actually gone, but

it turned out later that they went to the social and scientific room where all the sewing machines and big tables are. Mrs Limond had already put lots of old costumes there and they're going to turn some of them into new ones. But they're making some of them from scratch too and Ellie had to start pinning out patterns and cutting out fabrics straight away. It sounds pretty awful to me, like being in some sort of sweatshop, but Ellie seemed to love it for some strange reason. I suppose for her it's like as if I had to be someone's drumming assistant. Which would be lots of fun, really.

Cass and I kindly sneaked away when rehearsal was over, so Alice and her new love could be alone together. We are going to go into town to split a hot chocolate tomorrow. I didn't talk to anyone else on my way out.

SATURDAY ☺

My mother is a tyrant! I told her that I was going to meet Cass in town and she said, 'Oh no, you're not.'

'What do you mean?' I said. 'Have you grounded me without telling me? I haven't done anything! Anything grounding-worthy, I mean.'

My mother sighed like she was some sort of long-suffering saint, instead of an evil dictator.

'I haven't grounded you,' she said. 'We're going to see Daisy's new baby today. I told you about this ages ago.'

Daisy is my godmother. She is also one of my mum's oldest friends and she had a baby a few weeks ago. I do remember that, but I have no memory of mum telling me about this visit.

'But what about Cass?' I said.

'You can just tell Cass you forgot you were meant to be visiting someone who has always been lovely to you,' said Mum. 'Don't you want to see Daisy's baby?'

It's true, Daisy is lovely. She's a few years younger than my mum – they grew up on the same street – and she's like an honorary aunt. In fact, she's nicer than some of my actual aunts (like Auntie Celine, dad's sister, who says things like 'Aren't you very scrawny, Rebecca? You'd barely know you were a girl!' while pointing at my lack of chest). I was not so sure I wanted to see Daisy's baby, though. Apart from the fact that she's got two older kids already who are quite annoying, in my experience babies are very cute until you actually pick them up and then they go into fits of rage until you give them back to their parents.

Anyway, obviously I had no choice about going to see this baby because my mother was probably going to force me into the car if I refused, so I had to ring Cass and then we all went off to Daisy's house. It actually was nice to see her, though the baby started shrieking as soon as it saw me. And later it got sick on me. I don't think babies like me very much. Maybe it is because of my asymmetrical face? And the baby's older siblings were being bratty and having tantrums so what with the screaming baby and the shouting kids it was all a bit stressful.

But on a more positive note, Daisy reviews plays for work and she said she will come and see the musical! Not for work, obviously. But it is exciting that someone who knows a lot about the theatre will be there. My parents don't count. They clearly still think their insane production of *The Pirates of Penzance* was the greatest show ever staged.

Actually, I should have asked Daisy about that today. I bet Mum made her go and see it. I could have found out the truth about the show. I am sure Dad's solo 'pirate jazz ballet dance' did not go down as well with the audience as he and Mum say it did.

LATER

I think I am getting quite good at making up poems. Here is a haiku I wrote about Vanessa. Haikus are special Japanese poems with just seventeen syllables. They are great because they are very short and of course they don't have to rhyme.

Why does Vanessa
Act like such an idiot?
It's a mystery.

SUNDAY

Alice truly is a noble friend! She has made a big effort to show that she is not going to abandon her old chums even though she is in a blissful loved-up state now. She was getting a lift to meet Richard in town today, but she got her dad to call in to my house on the way so she could drop in my snare drum to me as a lovely surprise! How thoughtful of her. I have been missing my drums quite a bit and had wondered about getting my snare here so I could play it on its own, but I didn't want to mention it to Alice what with her being (literally) the injured party. It felt a bit mean to go 'So, I know you can't play your own instrument, but could you lug a bit of mine over to my house?' But she thought of it all by herself! Truly she is a better person than me. I hope she had a nice afternoon with Richard (I am not so bad really).

I had a great time bashing away on my snare this afternoon. Obviously it's not the same as having the whole kit, but it's still pretty cool. Of course, my parents gave out to me for making lots of noise. I don't give out to them when they're hooting and hollering with laughter going on about that musical of theirs, do I?

Well, I suppose I do, sometimes. But still.

MONDAY

Sort of bad, sort of good news at rehearsal today. I am no longer Karen's understudy. This is because Cathy and Ms Byrne are totally panicking because the show is on in a couple of weeks and we're already quite behind schedule. So they said they don't have time to rehearse the understudies properly.

'You'll just all have to make sure you don't get sick,' said Cathy sternly to the principal actors. She was doing her powerful stare. 'In fact, unless you're actually in hospital or dead, I want you on that stage and ready to go on the opening night.'

I think that even if Vanessa was in hospital she'd escape with a drip in her arm rather than miss her moment of glory. To hear the way she talks you'd think she was starring in a big play in the west end of London not a school musical.

In a way, I am very disappointed because, of course, there was always a tiny chance that Karen would be struck with a hideous illness and I would get a chance to shine. (I would also get to witness Karen's hideous illness, which I have to admit wouldn't bother me much). But in another, I am quite relieved that I don't have to bother 'observing her performance'. In fact, I can just ignore her from now on, which is fine by me. I couldn't take more of her 'helpful advice' or her going on about the latest stupid thing Bernard the Fairytale Prince (and Oscar-winning actor, practically, if you believe the way she talks about him) has said about how great she is. I am seriously starting to wonder if she really is going out with him. I'm starting to think she's made it all up. No one could be that devoted to Karen, surely?

Anyway, I don't think there's a chance the lead actors will

miss the show. They're all terrified of Cathy now. She looks so small and pretty, but even the boys don't dare disobey her. She is very charismatic. Jessie told me that whenever any of the main cast mess about or don't listen to her, she just stares silently at them in a terrible, disapproving way until they're intimidated into behaving. Jessie says Sam, the boy who's playing Uncle whatsisname, looked like he was going to burst into tears the last time Cathy did it to him.

TUESDAY ☾

I needn't have worried about Alice raving on about Bike Boy. She is very restrained and sensible. She only mentions him like, once every five minutes (I have a horrible feeling that when I was going out with Paperboy properly I mentioned him every second). You can just tell she's happy. No, what we should have worried about was Ellie and Mrs Limond. Ellie won't shut up about how wonderful Mrs Limond is and how she is her new idol.

'She makes clothes by hand!' she says. 'And they're amazing! She showed me loads of the old costumes and they're like something out of a film! And she made them all! With just a bit of help from girls like me. She's going to teach me how to do it and then I can be a fashion designer! It's like a dream come true!'

'But Ellie,' said Cass, 'doesn't Mrs Limond wear a giant fur coat in the manner of Cruella De Vil? I thought you were a vegetarian!'

Ellie looked a bit uncomfortable but then she said, 'I know, but that coat is, like, vintage now. She got it new back in the '60s. Those minks would have died of old age by now anyway.'

I am not sure this is a very vegetarian spirit.

WEDNESDAY

I replied to Paperboy's mail today. It was actually harder than I thought it would be. I told him I was really busy with the musical and told him about all the madness there, and about Alice and Bike Boy. And I told him about Vanessa's party, even though that seems like years ago now. But anyway, that was all quite easy and fun to write about it. But after that I didn't really know what to say. I was going to say that I missed him because I do, but not the same awful aching way I used to. I think I have got used to being without him. But you can't say that to someone, can you?

Anyway, he mightn't care one way or another. If he really missed me, he wouldn't have left it so long to mail me.

Boy so far away
I think you have forgotten
Poor old Rebecca.

I think I am getting quite good at writing poems. But I should probably branch out from the haikus; they feel like cheating because they are so short (they are quite fun, though). I might try writing a story again. I wish my friends were into writing stuff so I could talk about it properly to them. But the only person I know who likes writing is John Kowalski, and I barely know him. I haven't really talked to him all week. But he did wave at me across the rehearsal room this evening.

THURSDAY

I don't believe my parents. I was just watching telly in the sitting room with Rachel when my mother came in and just sort of hovered in the doorway. Finally she said, 'Rebecca, have you done your homework yet?'

Now, it wasn't exactly a lie when I said 'yeah' because I had read part of a poem for Mrs Harrington earlier.

But Mum said, 'Don't lie to me, Rebecca, you've been in here since you got home. You haven't had time to do anything. Off you go and do some work! You can watch TV later.'

I have never heard anything so unfair.

'How come I have to go and work while Rachel can sit there watching telly?' I cried.

'Because Rachel is not spending every evening at musical rehearsals instead of doing her homework. Now off you go! Upstairs!'

So I had no choice but to leave. I am not doing any homework though, I am writing this diary. So there, Mother! You can force me into this prison but you can't force me to read poems for Mrs Harrington!

Though I suppose I should read them, we're going to have to do something about them in class tomorrow.

LATER

I have done all my stupid homework now. And what thanks did I get from my mother when I went down to tell her it was all done? None!

'You shouldn't expect thanks and praise for just doing your homework,' she said. 'You're meant to be doing it! It's not a favour to me!'

Parents are never satisfied, no matter what you do. You'd think Emma's parents would be pleased about her doing that computer class because that's all very educational but no! They're now giving out to her for spending too much time on the computer at home, even though she's using it to write some sort of complicated computer code to create a computer that can think for itself.

Apparently, this is what the most advanced scientists in the world are trying to do, so if they haven't managed it I am not sure a fourteen-year-old is going to figure it out, even if she did go to a computer summer camp last year. But she says she might spot something they haven't.

I can't believe anyone's parents would be annoyed because their daughter is a scientific genius. But maybe they are worried that computers really will become more powerful than humans and take over the world? If so, then I suppose their annoyance is fair enough.

SATURDAY ☺

Very boring day. My parents are keeping up their new reign of terror and said I couldn't go down to Cass's house because I had to study. I pointed out that I didn't go out last weekend because they forced me to go and see a baby who got sick on me, but they said they didn't care. Mum said I was out practically every evening during the week, so I'd got to do some studying at the weekend. I told her and Dad that I am not out socialising during the week but working hard at a great theatrical project (we worked so hard at the rehearsal last night that poor Alice barely got to say a word to her new love Bike Boy and I didn't get a chance to speak to anyone apart from Alice), but they didn't care.

Well, they can make me stay at home, but they can't force me to do boring Irish homework. I am going to play the drums for a while instead.

LATER

Oh my God, my mum just came in and TOOK MY DRUM-STICKS! She says she is going to hide them unless I work for at least an hour. This is an outrage!

I suppose I might as well go and start the essay due in to Mrs Harrington on Wednesday. But just because I feel like doing it. Not because my mother wants me to.

MONDAY

Strange things are happening in our class. Usually Ellie's hair is all wild and flowing free because of her hippie upbringing, but today she came into school with the front of her hair all puffed up like Mrs Limond's. She is truly obsessed. And it's not even like Mrs Limond is particularly nice to her; she's practically made Ellie her slave! She seems to just bark orders at her all the time and Ellie does whatever she says. And she still calls Ellie 'Eleanor'.

We have started having fittings for costumes – Mrs Limond is re-using some of the 'men's' suits and things from previous years and she stuck a pin in poor Alice today. And she didn't even apologise. She just bellowed, 'Stop wriggling, child!' in her usual mad and posh fashion.

Luckily, Cathy and Ms Byrne aren't as psychotic as she is. Now the pressure of training understudies is off them they are quite cheerful. In fact, Ms Byrne said that us chorus people are 'coming along nicely'. We've been running through quite a few things with the main cast and it has all gone pretty well.

Also, today at the break I went out for a breath of fresh air and there was John Kowalski, moodily smoking a cigarette by the bikes. I was going to tell him you're not allowed to smoke on school grounds but when he saw me he smiled and said, 'Ah, hello, Miss Rafferty', and I forgot what I was going to say. So I said, 'Oh hello, I was just getting fresh air. It's quite stuffy in there.'

'I agree,' said John, taking a drag of his evil cancer-stick.

It's a bit ridiculous that he thought it was too stuffy so he decided he'd go and breathe in some noxious poison instead. I knew I should despise him for it, but somehow I couldn't. I could have done without the smell, though.

'I needed to get away,' he said. 'There's only so much of Vanessa I can stand.'

I knew I liked him for a reason.

'How's your writing going?' I asked.

'Not bad,' he said. 'I entered a student playwright competition so I'm waiting to see if I got on the shortlist.'

I asked if the play was a musical, inspired by our current

amazing project. He looked a bit put out.

'No,' he said. 'It's about a soldier about to go into battle who wonders whether he should kill himself rather than take an enemy's life.'

'Oh,' I said. Really I should have known it'd be something serious like that.

'So,' said John, looking more cheerful. 'How about you? Have you been writing any great works of art?'

'Well, not really,' I said. 'Just a few poems.'

'There's no such thing as JUST a few poems,' he said. 'You're making art. That's very impressive.'

Then we had to go back to the hall. I would have liked to stay there longer. Although I am not sure what I would have said about my poems. Most of them so far are about Paperboy or how annoying Vanessa is. He might have thought I was a bit mad.

WEDNESDAY

Rehearsal was great today! We were doing 'A Spoonful of Sugar', and at first Ms Byrne was getting a bit crotchety because we couldn't get the harmonies right and people kept coming in doing the whistling bits at the wrong time. But then it was like something clicked and it all came together and it sounded really good. It was like the band when we finally figured out how to play a song from beginning to end. It was brilliant, even though we have to sing it behind Vanessa and Karen (and Wiktoria Nowak from 2:4 who's playing Jane, the other kid, but she seems pretty nice so I don't have anything against her) while they parade about in front of us.

John Kowalski came up to me afterwards.

'Well, Miss Rafferty,' he said. 'You're nailing those chorus songs.'

'Ooh, thanks,' I said.

'Keep up the good work,' he said, and walked off. There's something so dashing about him. I wish he didn't smoke. Not that really it makes any difference to me whether he does or doesn't, of course. I'm just concerned for his health.

LATER

Oh. I just got a mail from Paperboy and I don't know how I feel about it.

He didn't break up with me. And I know he still likes me.

But I think he thinks we both need to move on. Actually, I don't just think that, I know it because he basically said it. He said, and I quote, 'I really miss you, but I want to know you're having a great life in Dublin while I'm having a great life over here. I don't want you to be sad just because I'm not coming back to Ireland. And I hope we both keep moving on and doing cool new stuff.'

I know he is right. I think I've known he was right for a while. But think I might have a cry now.

THURSDAY

I told Cass and Alice about Paperboy's mail (it doesn't count as moping and whining when something big or new happens). They were very understanding.

'It's not like he's broken up with you,' said Alice. 'He just knows you haven't been happy with, you know, the current situation between you and him. And I mean, you haven't.'

'It's true,' said Cass. 'I know it's ... I mean, I know it makes you feel a bit awful. But weren't you feeling awful before too?'

They are both right. Who knew both of them could be so wise? But at the same time I feel very sad. Sadder than I have in weeks.

Although they do have a point. I still don't feel quite as miserable as I did before the musical started. But I do feel more miserable than I did yesterday morning. I tried writing some poetry to cheer myself up, but it didn't work. I think I will just lie on my bed for a while and listen to music. If I lie down, I won't be able to see that stupid Mulligan kid across the road even if she does start dancing at me.

FRIDAY ☺

Had another big chat with John Kowalski today. He doesn't know anything about the Paperboy business so it is nice and distracting talking to him. Cass had to stay late after rehearsal because the paint wasn't dry on some of the carousel horses. I have to give Cass credit, she's turned out to be pretty good at set designing. So her dream wasn't really so illogical. She came up with a great idea for the 'Let's Go Fly a Kite' scene at the end – they've made big cardboard kites painted in cool patterns and put them on sticks, and we're all going to raise them up and down in formation. A bit like a synchronised dance (one of my own dreams, as you may remember).

Anyway, the rehearsal went pretty well this evening, even

though Vanessa kept asking John to go through lines with her, and we had so much to do I actually didn't really think about Paperboy at all during it. And then when it was finished, I was halfway up the school drive all on my own (I had kindly let Alice go ahead of me with Bike Boy) when a voice from behind me said, 'Hello there, Rafferty.'

Not even a Miss or a Ms. I didn't mind though. I actually liked it.

'Hey,' I said. 'How are you?'

'Oh, you know,' said John. 'A bit bored. Counting down the seconds until I never have to sing a song with Vanessa again.'

'Ouch,' I said. 'It's bad enough being her backing singers.'

'Oh well,' said John. 'It's all for the greater good. I think. It's an experience, anyway. And it's important to experience lots of weird things if you really want to be a writer. Maybe I'll write a play about her and what a scary diva she is.'

'She'd probably want to play herself,' I said.

'Good point,' said John thoughtfully. 'And if it showed her in a bad light, I bet she wouldn't even realise it. She doesn't really understand criticism, does she?'

'She really doesn't,' I said. 'She's unstoppable.' And I told him about her party. He was amazed.

'Wow,' he said. 'It sounds hideous. The vulgarity! It's almost so awful it's brilliant. Like a sort of pageant.'

'It was just awful for most of it,' I said. 'Especially for Alice.'

'What?' said John. 'Oh yeah, the wrist thing. Yeah, I suppose that's bad.'

'We probably would have never taken part in the musical if she hadn't hurt her wrist, though,' I said. 'And I'm glad we did. Not that it's worth Alice being hurt, obviously. But you know what I mean.'

'I do,' said John. 'I think it's a good thing too. You lot doing the musical.'

'Oh,' I said. I could feel my cheeks going pink.

'Yeah,' said John. 'It's done Richard good, going out with Alice. I think it's really enhanced his performance as Bert. It's like he's got a new drive, you know? A new vision.'

'Oh,' I said flatly.

'Yeah,' said John. 'And of course, I'm glad I met you.' He paused. 'Always good to meet a fellow writer.'

'Oh!' I said. We were at the corner of Gracepark Road now. John looked at his watch.

'Ah,' he said. 'I'd better run. My parents are making me go to my cousin's engagement party, or something. I wasn't really listening because they're so boring. Some stupid thing in a tacky hotel on the southside.'

He smiled. His mouth goes up more on the left side than the other when he smiles.

'Bye, Rafferty,' he said. And then he was off down Grace-park Road and I just stood there staring after him.

It wasn't until I got home that I thought about Paperboy and remembered his mail. The whole musical thing really has been a good distraction. I feel a bit better now, so I am going to watch telly and eat biscuits. Luckily, my parents were feeling lazy tonight and got a posh takeaway, so I wasn't forced to chop onions or something equally dreadful. For once. I'm sure they'll be making me slave away as usual tomorrow.

SATURDAY ☺

Quite a relaxing day today, which is just what I need after all the emotional upheaval and drama of the last week. Something must have happened to my parents. Not only did they not drag me out of bed at an ungodly hour and force to me to study/go to the shops/visit a baby, but when Alice called in to visit me before going in to town to see Richard, my mother actually produced some biscuits! Nice biscuits too, not boring old digestives or something. It was very mysterious, but I'm not complaining.

Alice is in a good mood too. We had a good chat about stuff. Richard sounds really nice, so nice that it makes me feel a bit jealous and sad about all the Paperboy business. But Alice doesn't go on about him in an annoying way. And I made a big effort to stick to the rules and I didn't go on about Paperboy's depressing mail. I am surprised to realise it actually made me feel better talking about other stuff, like the musical and how good Bike Boy and John are in it, and school, and, of course, Bike Boy and his ways (Alice says he wants them to try and write some songs together). I told her about my poem writing (though of course I didn't show her any) and she was very enthusiastic.

'It's great practice for lyric writing for when we get the band going again,' she said.

I told her a lot of the poems were haikus and they are too short to be a song, but she said it didn't matter.

'You're building up your artistic skills,' she said.

'That's kind of what John said,' I said. 'He told me he's writing a play. Oh, and he also said Vanessa was doing his head in.'

'I don't think she knows that,' said Alice. 'She keeps trying to corner him.'

'I know,' I said. 'It's really annoying.'

Alice looked at me in a slightly odd way, but then she looked at her watch and realised she was going to be late to meet her true love Bike Boy. So off she went.

But we had had great biscuit feast. It is amazing what a difference just being distracted can make. I feel quite serene now and ready for a night of reading and watching DVDs. And I'm going over to Cass's tomorrow for a bit so that will stop me from moping for at least a couple of hours.

SUNDAY

Excellent day! I was having a nice quiet drum this morning when my mum, of all people, said something that gave me an idea.

'You know I really support your, um, drumming dreams,' she said. 'But I kind of miss the days when all your drums lived in someone else's house.'

And that's when I got the idea (after I had asked my rude mother to get out of my room). For once I had some credit on my phone so I rang Cass straight away.

'Cass!' I said. 'Would your parents mind if we took over your front room for a bit this afternoon?'

'Um, no,' said Cass. 'They've gone to one of Nick's stupid football matches. I refused to go. But why?'

And I told her my amazing idea.

'What if I carry over my snare drum to your house and we have a mini band practice with your piano? Obviously you can't make all the sounds from the keyboard, and I'll only have my snare and not a full kit, but it'd be something. It would be like a mini band practice and it'll keep the songs fresh in our minds.'

'Ooh,' said Cass. 'That is a good idea.' Then of course she got all dithery, like she does almost every time we suggested doing something new with the band. 'What if we actually have forgotten all the songs? It's been weeks and weeks!'

I told her not to be silly and that I'd be over in twenty minutes. Actually, it took longer than that because once I left the house and started carrying the drum down the road the edges of it kept digging into my fingers, so every so often I had to take a break and let it rest on a wall or something. But I got there in the end. And it's a good thing I did because it turned out we definitely were out of practice. But it all started coming back to us as the afternoon went on, even though Cass couldn't play her keyboard noises and I could only do some very basic drumming. And it reminded me of how much I love the band. By the time I lugged the drum home again I was singing all our songs in my head.

It's funny, sometimes when I think of Paperboy I feel all sad. But whenever I am doing something interesting I don't feel sad at all.

I think I might be getting ... not over him. I don't even want to do that. I don't want to have anything to get over. But I think I am getting better.

MONDAY ☼

Ugh, every time I think Mrs Harrington has forgotten about my mother she starts going on about her again. It's not as bad as last term when she was like a crazy stalker, but it's still quite bad. She obviously had a bright idea over the weekend because today when the class was finishing up she said, 'So Rebecca, are your parents coming to that musical of yours?'

'Um, yes,' I said.

'I don't suppose you know which night they're coming? The Friday or the Saturday?' she said.

'I don't know yet,' I said. 'I mean, it's not for a few weeks. Why?'

'Oh, I'd just love to get to meet your mammy at last,' said Mrs Harrington. 'I can tell her about my holiday a few years ago. My husband and I went around the country staying in places mentioned in your mammy's books.'

Good lord.

'Did he mind?' I said. 'Your husband, I mean.'

'Oh no,' said Mrs Harrington, looking surprised by the very idea. 'He's a big Rosie Carberry fan too!'

There is no way I am letting Mrs Harrington (and her possibly equally mad husband) loose on my mum if I can help it. Not because of my mum (she deserves it, if you ask me), but because it would just fuel Mrs Harrington's mania. I thought they were going to come face to face at the end of last term at the parent-teacher night, but, luckily, Mum had a terrible cold so only my dad went. Anyway, I'll just find out what day my parents are going and tell Mrs Harrington it's the other one. It's a bit mean, but it's for her own good.

Rehearsals are really heating up again. I was talking to John during the break (I went out for some fresh air while Alice was talking to Bike Boy and there he was. He really shouldn't smoke. Not only is it bad for him but he'll get into loads of trouble if he's caught) and he said he keeps dreaming about Mr Banks's songs. I can't believe it'll all be over in a few weeks. It seems like the musical is just our life now.

TUESDAY ☾

Daisy rang my mum this evening and I answered the phone. Because Mum was in the kitchen talking to Maria from round the corner who'd come over to drop over a shears or something (they always talk about gardening, so boring), I decided to ask Daisy about *The Pirates of Penzance*.

'Was it actually any good?' I said. 'I mean, do you remember it at all?'

I thought Daisy would say 'Yes, and it was ridiculous.' But no!

'Of course,' she said. 'It was spectacular!'

'Are you serious?' I said. 'Did Mum and Dad tell you to say that?'

'What?' she said, and I must admit she sounded genuinely

baffled. 'No! It really was brilliant! I thought both your parents would go into the theatre professionally afterwards.'

I couldn't believe it. But she swore she wasn't joking.

'Your mum brought real soul to the Pirate King,' she said. 'When she flew over the stage on a rope it was like poetry in motion. And your dad's dance solo was out of this world. He got a standing ovation.'

I am gobsmacked. I think they must all have been mad in the '80s. Maybe they were all on drugs. I mean, I've seen the photos. Not only that, but I KNOW MY PARENTS. I've seen my dad dancing at my cousin's twenty-first. There is no way anyone ever gave those moves a standing ovation. And I find it very hard to believe that my mum hanging from a rope with huge hair was poetry in motion. I am not sure I can take Daisy seriously as a theatre critic anymore.

WEDNESDAY

Miss Kelly has surprised us by telling us she is going to go to the musical. I thought she'd be boycotting it because it's using up so much energy, but no!

'I have to see what seems to have been distracting half my

class for the last few months,' she said grimly. 'God knows what useful information you've missed when you were thinking about rehearsals instead of listening to me. I hope all this singing and dancing is worth it, girls.'

What Miss Kelly doesn't appreciate is that we are learning other skills at rehearsals. Who would have thought a few weeks ago that Alice and I would turn into exemplary members of the chorus? We have become much more disciplined since the long-ago days when Cass could make us laugh just by looming up behind a cardboard car wearing a cactus on her head. Today when we were singing 'Spoonful of Sugar', Mrs Limond marched into the hall and flung off her giant fur coat and it landed on top of poor Ellie's head. She was completely covered in coat and it took about five minutes for her to get out from under it. And I barely laughed at all. I have clearly grown up a lot recently.

Mrs Limond really is kind of terrifying, I don't know why Ellie loves her so much. Ellie says that Mrs Limond is teaching her the ways of fashion, but I'm not sure how chucking coats over her is going to teach her anything. Weirdly, Mrs Limond seems to love John Kowalski and Bike Boy. 'You two young men have excellent posture!' she cried today. She was so loud we could hear her all the way over on the other side of the hall. 'You were born to wear suits!' She doesn't think I have excellent posture. Every time we have a fitting she tells me not to slouch.

'You're short enough as it is,' she said. 'I don't see why you want to make yourself look even shorter.'

She has a point, I suppose, but still.

Even though Mrs Limond is mad and rude, the costumes are looking pretty good. I've got a sort of generic olden-day dress because it works for being a nanny and a person at the races and all that, and an excellent hat which somehow fits over my stupid mad hair. I love my costume. And Bike Boy and John Kowalski really do look dashing in their suits. Much better than in boring old school uniforms. I wish we could just wear our costumes to school instead. I think it would make school much more interesting.

THURSDAY

Oh my God, I think the downtrodden minion uprising may have begun at last!

Today, at lunchtime, Karen and Vanessa were going on in

their usual annoying way about how hard they were working and how they needed to practise every hour of every day.

'My boyfriend Bernard has been a godsend,' said Karen, sounding about forty-five. You'd think she'd been married to Bernard for twenty years instead of going out with him for about two minutes. 'He really understands the work that goes into playing a leading role.'

'We still need to work on our lines,' said Vanessa. She turned to Alison and Caroline who were sitting there eating their lunches quietly.

'Hey,' she said. 'I've got an idea. Why don't you two help us with our lines now? It'll help me and Karen and give you two something fun to do. Let's go to the cloakroom now and go through the nursery scenes – you can have our scripts.'

'Great idea,' smarmed Karen. She and Vanessa got up to go.

But Alison and Caroline didn't move. They just looked at each other and then Caroline said, in quite a nervous voice, 'Actually, I think we're going to stay here and finish our lunch.'

Vanessa just stared at her.

'What?' she said.

Caroline looked even more nervous. But then Alison said, 'Yeah, we're just going to have our sandwiches. You go and practise, though. We'll see you later.'

Karen and Vanessa looked as if, I dunno, a chair had started speaking to them. I have to admit that Karen looked a bit awkward. Maybe she was remembering the time Alison defied her at the Battle of the Bands and knew she couldn't go too far. But Vanessa just looked annoyed. 'God, I can't believe you're both so selfish. You'd prefer to eat sandwiches than help the stars of the school make the musical even better. Well, we'd better practise anyway. Come on, Karen!' And off she marched. Karen looked like she was going to say something, but then she put her nose in the air and marched out after Vanessa.

I wanted to give Alison and Caroline a round of applause, but I didn't. I just looked at them and nodded in a pleased sort of way. In retrospect, I might have looked a bit odd. But I couldn't help it. I was delighted. The musical is truly bringing out the best in everyone. Even people who aren't actually in it, which is especially impressive.

Actually, now I come to think of it, it's definitely bringing out the worst in Karen and Vanessa. So maybe my theory is not correct. But still. It's bringing out the best in some of us, and that has to be good.

FRIDAY ☺

Oh dear, the minion uprising has not gone down well with Karen and Vanessa. They were both showing off more than ever at rehearsal today. I think it is to make up for the fact that their loyal sidekicks have rebelled (though they haven't rebelled very much, they were all sitting together at lunch today. Still, I didn't see Alison and Caroline helping the other two with their lines, so I am still hopeful. And Emma says that Alison is really good at the computer class so maybe she will start spending more time becoming a techie genius and forget about Karen).

Anyway, Vanessa and Karen were really awful. I feel so sorry for Wiktoria from 2:4, having to play Jane Banks, stuck between those two goons. She is looking more and more depressed as the rehearsals go on. I don't know how she's made it this far. If I had to share every single scene with Karen and Vanessa, I'd have run away weeks ago. It just shows what a trouper she is.

Actually, I think John Kowalski is really getting fed up with Vanessa. She was all over him again this evening. He was on his way out of the hall at the break (I'm afraid it was to smoke a cigarette) and Vanessa pounced on him.

'John!' she cried. 'Just who I was looking for. Tell me what you think of this dance step from the kite scene.'

And before John could do anything, she started hopping about the place with a hideous smirk on her face.

'Very nice,' he said when she eventually stopped. But he looked annoyed. 'Now, if you'll excuse me ...' And he marched off before she could say another word. But Vanessa looked very pleased with herself. I don't know why; it was obvious that he was trying to escape from her. I think.

I only talked to him for a second today, when he returned from his smoking session. As soon as he saw me, he smiled. I have to admit he has such a nice smile.

'Hey there, Rafferty,' he said. 'Back to the grindstone.' And then he had to go back to Cathy and the principals' rehearsals. I didn't see him afterwards because I was going over to Cass's house and we left before he did (Alice and Bike Boy were going on an actual date, sort of – just to a café down on Drumcondra Road).

'Are you okay?' said Cass when we were walking down Griffith Avenue. 'Any more news from Paperboy?'

'Um, no,' I said. 'I haven't mailed him back yet.'

Cass looked surprised.

'Seriously?' she said.

'Yeah,' I said. 'I haven't been sure what to say.'

'Hmm,' said Cass. 'Well, what do you want to say to him? Apart from, like, come home from Canada.'

'I dunno,' I said. 'I mean, I actually see what he means. I kind of know he's right. But I don't want to say "Fine, let's break up." That's so final. It's awful.'

'But you don't have to say that,' said Cass. 'I mean, you can just say something about wanting him to be happy too. That's nice and vague and he won't think you're sitting around moping.'

Cass looked very wise, which is quite unusual for her. I reminded her about my rule to stop moping. At least in public.

'Oh yeah,' said Cass. 'You've been very good so far. I mean, you haven't moped for ages. Not at me, anyway.'

'Thanks,' I said.

'Are you sure your lack of moping has nothing to do with a certain ... someone?' said Cass. Now she did not look very wise. She had a big stupid grin on her face. 'A moody someone with floppy hair?'

'No!' I said. 'If by someone you mean John Kowalski. We're

just friends. Anyway, he smokes.'

'He could give up,' said Cass.

'It doesn't matter whether he does or not,' I said. 'Because it has nothing to do with me. I haven't actually broken up with Paperboy. So how could I want to do anything with John Kowalski?'

'The human heart is a mysterious thing,' said Cass in a ridiculous voice. She is definitely not wise. In fact, she was talking a lot of rubbish. Anyway, we stopped talking about my love life (or lack of it) because we had reached Cass's house. When we were settled in her bedroom (which is still so much nicer than mine it depresses me. By the time my parents agree to do mine up again I'll be old enough to leave home) Cass told me about her and Liz's new idea. They are talking about doing a musical side-project.

'Just keyboards and bass,' she said. 'Liz's big sister has a bass she can use.'

I got a bit worried then.

'Cass,' I said, 'I hope you are not forgetting Hey Dollface in all this. I mean, I hope you're not going to get obsessed with your new band and abandon us when Alice's wrist is better.'

Cass looked outraged at the suggestion.

'Of course not!' she said. 'As if I would. This is just for fun, for me and Liz.'

Cass is a terrible liar, so I think she must have been telling the truth. Which means Hey Dollface is safe. It was a fun evening anyway. Cass's mum made us a delicious lasagne and afterwards we went back to her room and danced around to very loud music until Cass's annoying little brother Nick came in and turned the volume down. Everyone's siblings are annoying, Alice is so lucky being an only child.

SATURDAY ☺

I replied to Paperboy's mail today. I followed Cass's advice and was quite vague. I said there was no need to worry about me. I was doing loads of cool stuff and I was having great fun on the musical. Which is actually all true. I said I'd made new friends and I was glad he had new friends too. And I thought moving on was a good thing. Which is also all true. If I had been very brave I would just have written 'Are we actually going out anymore?' But I'm not so I didn't.

SUNDAY

I am not the only one suffering because of romance. Poor Alice is as well. Not because there is anything wrong between her and Bike Boy – he clearly really likes her, and she really likes him, so that's okay. It's just the fact that Alice lives out in the middle of nowhere. She has to get lifts everywhere because they live, like, two miles from the nearest bus stop. Luckily, her parents don't mind giving her lifts and their jobs are quite flexible so they can pick her up from school and rehearsal, but it doesn't always suit them and it was a huge hassle just going to a café in Drumcondra after the rehearsal on Friday. We were just on the phone for ages and she said that Bike Boy is very understanding about it but she wishes she could just casually arrange to meet him in town like I could with Paperboy in those long-ago days.

I suppose I should be grateful that my parents decided to buy a house in a fairly central location. Though it is hard to be grateful to them for anything. Today Mum was in one of her annoying 'caring parent' moods and started asking me questions about my Life. Which I did not want to talk to her about.

'You do seem more cheerful recently,' she said. 'How are things with ...?'

But before she could continue, I said, 'They're fine! Everything's fine!'

'Oh,' she said. 'Well, good. You do know you can always come to me if there's anything seriously wrong, don't you?'

'There isn't!' I said.

'Good,' she said. Then she didn't say anything and I hoped she was going to go away again, but no. Instead, she said, 'You know, very few people keep going out with their first boyfriend or girlfriend forever. Most people don't meet the person they want to spend their lives with until they're much, much older.'

'You met Dad when you were in college,' I said.

'Yes, but (a) there is a big difference between being twenty and fourteen and (b) I didn't even go out with him until a few years after we graduated,' she said. 'I met him in third year when I came back from America and then we did the musical. But we were just friends for ages and ages.'

'What, you mean you agreed to go out with him after seeing him in that musical?' I said.

'He was very good in that musical!' she said indignantly.

'Very attractive, if you must know. His dancing was amazing. I think, in retrospect, I had a little bit of a crush on him even then.'

'Oh my GOD, Mother,' I said. 'I am not talking about this for one minute longer.'

And I marched upstairs and put some music on. I really do not know which is worse, her treating me like a servant or trying to be nice to me.

MONDAY

Cass has cut her hair! Like, really cut her hair! Instead of shoulder-length sort of layered, sort of fringey golden brown hair she now has a proper fringe and a wavy bob. She got it done on Saturday and said she was dying to ring me and Alice yesterday and tell us about it, but she thought she would surprise us. Which she did.

'I can't believe you have actually chosen a fringe,' said Alice. 'I mean, you've been trying to grow yours out for ages and ages.'

'I just thought I should embrace the fringe,' said Cass. 'It's clearly my destiny. And then something came over me, and I thought, I want a bob! And the hairdresser said it was a good idea.'

Even John Kowalski noticed Cass's hair and he never seems to pay much attention to other people.

'Your friend Cass looks different,' he said when we were chatting during the break and Cass was climbing a wobbly ladder with a paint pot hanging dangerously from one hand. 'Cool hair.'

It does look really cool. And it sort of goes with her glasses, even though she still says she hates her glasses. She looks really pretty. In fact, I am a bit jealous. My hair still looks wavy and weird.

Anyway, when John wasn't praising Cass's hair we had a good conversation about what we want to do in college. I haven't really thought much about college, apart from, of course, knowing that I want to go. And I suppose I want to do some sort of arts degree. I just can't decide what. I'd thought about English, but maybe I should try for drama too, now that I've really discovered my theatrical side. Anyway, it doesn't matter if I don't really know exactly what I want to do because I've got three years to think about it, but when I said that John looked appalled.

'But Rafferty,' he said. 'You've got to make a plan. And a back-up plan. You've got to have a vision!'

Heavens.

'Well, what are you going to do?' I asked.

'I've got several options,' said John. 'I'm just weighing them up. There's drama in Trinity or UCD, but maybe I'll do English and drama. And I'm also considering applying for Rada in London.'

'What's Rada?' I said.

'R.A.D.A. The Royal Academy of Dramatic Art,' said John, looking slightly surprised that I didn't already know. Anyway, it turns out Rada is, like, incredibly posh and prestigious and loads of really famous, serious actors went there. It's so fancy, it sounds like you're basically taught by the Queen. John thinks it would help him hone his theatrical skills for his future as a famous writer/actor/director person.

I wonder if I could get in there myself? I didn't say that to him, though, in case he thought I was, like, copying him like a weirdo and I was going to follow him across the Irish Sea. I just nodded and went back to the rehearsal. But I have been thinking of it ever since. Just imagine me and John as glamorous young student actors in London. 'Who are that attractive young Irish couple?' people would ask. Not that we would be a couple-couple, of course. Just friends. And actorly colleagues.

WEDNESDAY

Ended up walking down the road with John Kowalski again because Cass's piano lesson was moved around and she had to leave rehearsal early. Somehow we keep finding ourselves leaving at the same time. We had a very interesting conversation about life and books and our dreams of the future. John Kowalski's parents sound even worse than mine.

'They just care about money and trivial things,' he said. 'I can't stand their inane chatter.'

My parents are also full of inane chatter at the moment. If I never hear the words 'Pirates of Penzance' again, it'll be too soon.

John is an only child. I asked him if he wished he had brothers and sisters but he said no, he was glad he hadn't.

'I need time to myself to write,' he said. 'Siblings would be a distraction.'

I can't argue with that. I was trying to write a story this

evening and Rachel stomped in roaring about something stupid. She says I've used up her posh Chanel lipstick and she knows it was me because she hasn't used it for weeks and it's gone down loads in its tube (has she been measuring it? I wouldn't put it past her). She's such a miser. I've barely used it myself, I just let other people use it at Vanessa's party. Quite a lot of people, in retrospect. I won't tell her that, though.

Actually, maybe it was a good thing she burst in and stopped me writing because I'm not sure my story was much good. I was trying to write a serious story about a young actress, but I kept thinking of funny things to put in. Which is not good if you are trying to be a serious writer. And I am. Trying to be one, I mean. I'm pretty sure there is no room for funniness in great art. John doesn't seem to think there is, anyway. He thinks great art is about war and passion and, I dunno, dying and stuff. Not stupid jokes.

THURSDAY

All the teachers can't wait until the musical is finished. Even Mrs Harrington seemed a bit impatient today.

'I know it's very exciting, girls,' she said. 'I'm looking forward to it myself. But we've got to remember school comes first!'

But it was Miss Kelly who got most annoyed. I suppose you can't blame her really. When she came into the classroom today Alice and I were showing people how we act while singing and it was a bit noisy.

'You can do whatever you like in your rehearsals,' bellowed Kelly. 'But when you're in this classroom you're here to work, not fool around!'

Actually, I think that when we're in her classroom, we're there to be terrified rather than work, but none of us said that.

'I will be keeping a special eye on all of you musical girls,' Kelly went on, 'to make sure you're keeping up with the class.'

She pointed at Ellie, who looked a bit scared.

'What are you doing in this show?' she demanded.

'Um, costumes. With Mrs Limond.'

And then something surprising happened. I kind of assumed Kelly would think Mrs Limond was a frivolous person for being so devoted to fashion, but no! She thinks Mrs Limond is an environmental heroine!

'You could all learn from Mrs Limond, girls,' she cried. 'That woman has made all her own clothes since 1952. She's not supporting the pointless consumerism that's destroying the environment! And she's been recycling school costumes for years. Last year she turned a Russian peasant dress from the 1997 production of *Fiddler on the Roof* into one of Sandy's dresses in *Grease*. She's a recycling inspiration to us all! Isn't she, Ellie?'

'Um, yes,' said Ellie, looking a bit stunned.

The thought of Mrs Limond recycling old costumes cheered Miss Kelly up no end, so the rest of the class was fine, really. Well as far as the musical goes. There was still a lot of environmental disaster and rants about which countries contribute most to our impending doom, but we're used to that now.

FRIDAY ☺

Oh my God!

John Kowalski kissed me. And I kissed him back.

I am an adulterer!

Okay, I am not technically an adulterer as I am obviously not married. And it's not like Paperboy and I are going out properly anymore. In fact, we are meant to be moving on. But still! We never officially broke up! Oh dear.

This is what happened. There was some sort of prop emergency, so Cass and her team were staying on a bit later after rehearsal again. When we were getting our stuff together, Alice and Bike Boy were gazing into each other's eyes in a way that made me feel very left out (I mean, I really am happy for her and everything, but it doesn't mean I want to stand there and, like, gawp at the two of them). So I just slipped out of the hall and somehow I found myself walking out with John Kowalski.

Well, by 'somehow' I mean that I was walking out of the hall and he came up to me and said, 'Hello, Rafferty. How's life in the chorus?'

And I said, 'Oh, you know. Chorus-y.'

'Ah,' said John Kowalski. 'What a surprise.' He paused. 'Are you hanging around waiting for anyone or are you going home now?'

'Home now,' I said.

'What a coincidence,' he said. 'So am I.'

And we walked out of school and up the drive together. I have to admit I had a funny feeling that something was going to happen, but I wasn't sure what.

'You know that play I wrote that I told you about?' he said.

'The one about the soldier who can't decide whether or not to kill himself?' I said.

'Yes,' he said. 'Well, I got a mail yesterday saying I was on the shortlist. The winner will be announced in a couple of weeks.'

'Wow,' I said. 'That's brilliant.'

'Yeah,' said John Kowalski. 'I knew I just had to get it out there.' He looked at me. 'Some day, Rafferty, I'm going to work in the theatre, and I'm going to be famous.' He looked like there was a fire inside him. 'I know I am.'

'And when you are, you can get Hey Dollface to do the music for all your plays,' I said.

He laughed. 'I can do the music myself, thanks very much! If music is needed, of course. But thanks.'

'I can't decide whether I'd like to be in a band full time or not,' I said. 'I mean, I kind of want to. But then I want to be a writer. And I do sometimes think of being an actress. Especially after all this musical stuff.'

I thought John Kowalski might say something like, 'You can be my leading lady!' But he didn't.

'Well, you'd better decide,' he said. 'There's no time to waste. You've got to follow your muse. Just make sure it's the right one.'

'That's easier said than done,' I said. 'Maybe I'll just, um, follow the band muse for a while. Once Alice is better, of course.'

'You should play the guitar instead of her,' said John. We were nearly at the corner now.

'No!' I said. 'I mean, I can't play it at all.'

'You could learn,' said John. We had reached the corner now and it was freezing cold and the wind was crazy, but we both just stood there. 'You can do anything you want.'

'I'm not sure,' I said, 'that I actually want to learn.'

'But wouldn't you prefer to be out in front playing the guitar?' he said. 'Isn't that more glamorous? And exciting?' Without me really knowing how, he had moved quite close to me. He's so much taller than me it was like he was protecting me from the wild wind.

'Well yes,' I said. 'But I love drumming. It's very satisfying hitting things with sticks.'

'Oh, Rafferty,' he said. We were very close together now. 'You're not like any girl I've ever met.'

And then he kissed me! And I didn't pull away and go, 'No, John Kowalski, you can't kiss me for I love another, and he is far away in Canada.' I didn't even hesitate for a second. I just kissed him back. I couldn't help myself.

And ... it was really good. It wasn't exactly the same as kissing Paperboy. He tasted of cigarettes but, after a moment, I didn't mind. He was a bit more stubbly and scratchy, but that was kind of nice. He was a very good kisser too – not that I have anyone to compare him with but Paperboy. It all felt very passionate. Maybe that is because it is a forbidden love. Not that it is love, of course. Is it lust? That is a bit shocking.

Anyway, it went on for ages too. At least it felt like ages. It was like time wasn't going at its normal speed. I could have stayed there all day but, after a while he pulled away and smiled at me and said, 'God, Rafferty, I don't know what came over me. Want to do that again?'

I couldn't say anything. I just nodded. And then we were, well, kissing again. Until my phone rang.

'Oh God,' I said. 'I bet that's my mum. Um, I'd better go.'

'If duty calls,' drawled John Kowalski. He smiled at me. How could I have ever wondered whether he was good-looking or not? 'See you on Monday, Rafferty.' And he strode off down the road in his magnificent coat and I stared after him before remembering I'd better answer my phone or Mum would be convinced I'd been murdered and would send out some sort of search party.

But now Paperboy isn't the last person I've kissed. Now he isn't the only person I've kissed! It makes me feel like everything between us is really over. And that makes me feel sad.

But at the same time ... when John Kowalski kissed me, it was like I was melting. I suddenly fancied him so much my legs went all wobbly. How can I be so fickle?!

It really was amazing though. Even with the cigarette taste. Oh God.

I am going to have a lie down and a think.

LATER

I have thought. And I think I might be a bit in love with John Kowalski. But how can I love two boys at once?

Maybe I am not. Maybe I am really over Paperboy at last.

SATURDAY ☺

I told Rachel what happened last night. I couldn't help it, I needed to tell someone, and I couldn't bring myself to tell Cass and Alice. I know Rachel is annoying, but it's true that when it comes to the ways of love, she knows more about the world than I do. And for someone who seems to spend a lot of her time yelling at me for no real reason, she has been surprisingly nice about my romantic problems in the past.

So this morning I went into her room. She was lying on her bed, scribbling away in a notebook. Can she have a diary too? I can't believe she's been writing one and I don't know about it. I mean, you'd think I'd have found it by now; it's not like I don't have a quick look around her room every so often just to check out (and, okay, sometimes borrow) her make-up and CDs and stuff.

'God, what do you want?' she said, stuffing the notebook under her pillow. (It has to be a diary. If it was homework or something she wouldn't have bothered hiding it from my observant gaze.)

'Um, nothing,' I said. 'Except ...' Oh, it pained me to say this. I ended up mumbling it. 'I sort of want your advice.'

Rachel looked a lot more cheerful.

'Oh, you do, do you?' she said. 'About what?'

'Well,' I said, sitting down on the edge of her bed. (She has a much nicer duvet cover than I do. My parents STILL won't redecorate my room so my sheets and stuff are still all stupid babyish pinks and purples.) 'You know that boy John Kowalski who's doing the musical?'

'Who, the one who looks like a First World War solider?'

she said. I can't believe she thought that too. 'The same one you've been hanging around street corners with?'

'Hardly hanging around street corners,' I said. 'That sounds like we're in a gang or something!'

'Well, you've been hanging around at the corner of Gracepark Road often enough,' said Rachel. 'I've seen you from the other side of the road on my way home from Jenny's house.'

Sometimes I don't know why I bother talking to her, it's like she can't stop herself from tormenting me.

'God, that's just because we walk out of the rehearsals together sometimes and that junction is the point where I go one way and he goes another,' I said. 'We're just talking!'

'Yeah, right,' said Rachel, annoyingly. 'Anyway, yes, I do know him. Or at least I know who he is. What about him?'

'Well,' I said. 'Um. The thing is ...'

'Oh my God,' said Rachel. 'You snogged him, didn't you?'

'What?' I said. 'No! Well, yes.'

'Well, well, well,' said Rachel, and she looked so smug that I wished I hadn't said anything at all. 'I knew it. So, what happened?'

So I told her.

'And then he kissed me,' I said.

'Not like any girl I've ever met?' said Rachel. 'Well, I bet he's right about that. I'm joking! I'm joking! That's quite a romantic thing to say.'

It is, isn't it?

'So,' said Rachel. 'Do you like him?'

'Well, yes,' I said. 'Obviously. Or, y'know, I wouldn't have, like, gone along with the whole kissing thing. But I still feel terrible.'

'What?' said Rachel. 'Why?'

I couldn't believe I even had to tell her.

'Because of Paperboy!' I said.

Rachel sighed and suddenly went all grown up.

'Bex,' she said. 'I know you really miss him. But you know, in your heart of hearts that you weren't ever going to, like, stay going out with him forever, don't you? I mean, it's been months and months! And he's not coming back here! You don't have anything to feel guilty about!'

And I suppose I know that she is right. I don't know when I'm going to see Paperboy again. He told me to move on. And he's on the other side of the world (almost). And John Kowalski is right here, and he's not as obviously gorgeous as Paperboy, and he's not as friendly and cheerful, but he's so intelligent and interesting and intense and I know he's a bit arrogant, but he knows exactly what he wants to do and he's absolutely sure he can do it. And I can't help it, I really, really fancy him.

There! I've said it.

And it doesn't mean that I've forgotten about Paperboy. Because of course I haven't. But I know we're not really going out anymore, and the longer he's away, the less ... real he seems. And John Kowalski is real.

Anyway, Rachel was full of old lady wisdom about living in the moment (just like Alice and John Kowalski himself; it's like everyone is in league) and, yes, embracing life.

'Do you honestly, in your heart of hearts, think you are still properly going out with Paperboy?' she said. 'Do you think you can keep going out on either side of the world forever?'

And I said, 'Well ... no.'

'And do you like John?' she said. 'Like, do you think about him when he's not there, and are you all excited to see him, and does the thought of him being with someone else make you want to die?'

'Oh,' I said. 'Well yes. Sort of. Maybe not die, exactly.'

'And do you fancy him? Do you think he's actually attractive in a hot-boy sort of way?'

'I usen't to,' I said. 'I mean, I wasn't sure whether he was good-looking or not. But now I definitely do.'

'And is he, like, a decent human being?'

'God, did you ask yourself all this rubbish when you started going out with Tom?' I said.

'No,' said Rachel. 'But then, I wasn't torturing myself and making myself feel guilty for absolutely no reason.'

'Okay, okay,' I said. 'I do like him. I do!'

'Well then,' said Rachel. 'There's no problem. Go off and enjoy him.'

Can it really be that easy?

Maybe it can.

SUNDAY

Went over to Cass's this afternoon and told her about the JK incident.

'I knew it!' she said gleefully, 'I told you this would happen.'

Usually I hate it when Cass is right about something and I am wrong. But I didn't really care today. Cass, like Rachel, thinks I have no need to be guilty.

'Paperboy actually told you he didn't want you to, you know, live in the past!' she said. 'He WANTED you to move on! You know, I think you're so used to feeling miserable and sorry for yourself that you can't get used to being properly happy about something.'

I wouldn't have put it quite like that, but she had a point.

LATER

Rang Alice and told her all. She was all excited, at first, and she didn't think there was any, you know, adultery problems, but then she got a bit serious.

'You do like him as a person, don't you?' she said. 'Richard said he can be a bit moody. And he's, like, his friend.'

'Of course I like him!' I said. 'And he's not moody. He's just ... serious, some of the time. But he's really cool when you get to know him.'

Which he is.

'Well, as long as you're sure,' said Alice. 'You have to be careful.'

So one minute I have to stop moping over Paperboy and move on and the next I have to be careful of John Kowalski!

I just can't win!

Oh, all this romantic drama is very tiring. I feel very old and sophisticated now. I am going to lie on my bed and think about LIFE.

LATER

Got bored thinking about life and went down to watch telly.

MONDAY

I think I am sort of going out with John Kowalski, but I am not quite sure. There's something going on, anyway. I have to admit that when I arrived at rehearsal today I had a horrible fear that he was going to (a) ignore me or (b) be friendly but pretend nothing romantic had happened. It was soon pretty obvious that he wasn't going to ignore me because he nodded at me from across the hall as soon as he saw me, but he always does that anyway now, so that doesn't really mean anything. It meant that I was quite distracted for a lot of the rehearsal because I was wondering about him. On the plus side, this meant that Vanessa and Karen didn't annoy me too much.

But, on the downside, I sort of forgot what song we were singing and got given out to by Ms Byrne. I still haven't forgotten when she threatened to kick messers out of the chorus so I tried not to think about John after that.

Anyway, I didn't really know what to do, but during the break I went out to the loo and there he was in the corridor, presumably on his way back from SMOKING. Even that isn't enough to turn me off him. I really must fancy him.

'Ah,' he said, and for a moment my heart sank. But then he grinned and said, 'Hello, Rafferty. I've been thinking about you all weekend.'

'Oh?' I said in a sort of wobbly voice. 'Good things, I hope.'

'Oh yeah,' he said. And then he kissed me again! Just quickly but quite passionately. Then he turned to go back into the hall and said, 'Feel like walking down the road together after this is over?'

And I just nodded.

Anyway, when rehearsal was over I told Cass and Alice that I was walking out with John. I didn't want to just go off on them. That would be breaking my rules and I am still determined to stick to them in all this drama. But Cass and Alice are very understanding. Well, sort of. Cass said she was just relieved I wasn't still moping (my least favourite word). 'Go forth,' she said dramatically, 'with that strange play-writing boy.'

'He's not strange,' I said crossly.

'He is a bit,' said Cass. 'But there's nothing wrong with that.'

So off we went. I felt a bit awkward as we went down the road. I don't think he did. He always looks very confident, even when he looks all moody and serious. Eventually he said, 'So, Rafferty, this whole kissing thing that keeps happening between us. You want to keep doing it? Because I do.'

'Oh!' I said. 'Um, well. Yes.'

'Good,' he said. And kissed me again. The wind was blowing and it was dark and it all felt very dramatic, not like my normal life at all. We stayed talking for a while afterwards.

'You know,' said John. 'I think you and I are kindred spirits. We're not like everyone else. We care more about things. We have artistic temperaments.'

And then he kissed me again and then I went home.

Actually now I am home and thinking about it away from John's intense gaze, I have to admit that I am quite like some other people. I am quite like Cass and Alice, for example, otherwise they wouldn't be my best friends. But still, in a way, I think John could be right. Maybe I do have a unique artistic temperament. That would explain why I love drumming so much and why I can't help myself acting while I am singing in the musical. And even why I can't settle down in Mrs O'Reilly's class and I keep drawing pictures of Cass dressed as a peasant or Christopher Columbus or something. I am a free spirit! An artist who can't be tamed by society's conventions!

I think John Kowalski is opening my mind.

TUESDAY ☾

Why can't my parents just act like everyone else's parents? I was playing my drums this evening IN MY OWN ROOM and my mum stuck her head in the door.

'I'm not making too much noise!' I said. 'And besides, it's only half six. You can't stop me practising my drums! I need to play them! I'm … a free spirit!'

My mum looked quite offended.

'I wasn't going to give out to you,' she said. 'I was just thinking that drumming reminded me of a drum solo in *The Pirates of Penzance*. Ed! Come here!'

And a moment later my dad appeared.

'Go on, Bex,' said my mum. 'Play that beat again.'

I knew if I didn't, I'd be there all night with them nagging at me, so I did.

'Doesn't that sound like the extra drumming bit Joe added in the policemen's song to make it a bit more up to date?'

'Oh yeah!' said my dad. 'That was great. And then they both started marching around singing 'Taran-ta-ra, taran-ta-ra!' until I booted them out. And even then I could hear them laughing and singing downstairs.

God, they're such enormous freaks. Why can't they just be normal? It is very hard being a free spirit with them around.

WEDNESDAY

It is quite exhausting going out with John Kowalski. If we are actually going out. I am not quite sure. We are definitely kissing on a regular basis. And talking. It is all very intense. It is also quite different from me and Paperboy. We used to just sit around and laugh a lot. But John is not really into sitting around and laughing. After rehearsal today (which went very well – Ms Byrne actually PRAISED me and Alice for our acting-singing in 'I Love To Laugh') we went to a café on Drumcondra Road and talked about our visions for the world (I texted my mum and told her I was going for post-rehearsal tea in the café but I didn't tell her who I was going with).

'The country shouldn't be run by dull politicians, the way it is now!' John said, taking a drink of his pitch-black espresso. 'It should be run by artists and writers and dreamers!'

I expect that would be more exciting. Although a few of my parents' friends are artists and writers (and possibly dreamers) and I don't think they should be in charge of anything. Also, as I pointed out to him, my own tyrannical, embarrassing mother is a writer.

'She's bad enough when she's ruling my life,' I said. 'I don't think I'd like her ruling the entire country.'

'Oh, I don't mean writers like her,' he said. 'I mean proper writers.'

'She is a proper writer,' I said. 'I mean, she writes novels. She makes a living out of it!'

'A living!' he said scornfully, and laughed a hollow sort of laugh. 'As if making money from writing makes you a true artist.' According to him, a true artist doesn't care about something as mundane as money. I suppose that is true. I am quite glad my mother isn't that sort of writer, though. As she is so fond of reminding me and Rachel, we wouldn't have a house or an iPod each if she didn't earn money from her books. Dad certainly doesn't earn enough teaching students about history to pay for all that on his own.

Anyway, I like that John Kowalski is very passionate about everything. I can imagine us sitting in some sort of romantic place (I am not sure where. Definitely not my room – it's the most unromantic place on earth with its baby-ish decor), reading each other poetry. No one has ever read poetry to me before, but if anyone would do it, it would be him. I felt all wobbly when he kissed me goodbye at the corner of Gracepark Road. Who knew those traffic lights could look so romantic in the evening light?

THURSDAY

I have been working on my story this evening and, you know, I can see why Mum became a writer now. It really is fun making stuff up. Mum has always said it's hard work, but I never really believed her. How hard can a job be if you can do it in your pyjamas? I know for a fact that there are days when she doesn't get dressed properly until after eleven! Anyway, the only problem is that I am still trying to write a serious story, but whenever I read back over it, it doesn't feel serious at all. It's like I keep thinking of funny things to put in and then it's hard to make it serious again. It is very frustrating.

LATER

I suppose I could always ask Mum for writerly advice.

LATER

Oh God, I can't. Just imagine how smug she would be. I will just have to soldier on.

FRIDAY ☺

Today John Kowalski told me he doesn't like the terms boy-friend and girlfriend.

'Why formalise what we have, Rafferty?' he said today. 'Why tie ourselves down with labels?'

Which is fair enough, I suppose.

I told Cass this on the phone tonight and she was not impressed. 'If I had a girlfriend, or boyfriend, I wouldn't mind labelling them,' she said. 'It's not like you wanted to get his name tattooed across your forehead.'

I should hope not. But anyway, Cass has never had a very romantic soul. And John is very romantic, in a very exciting way. When we reached the corner of Gracepark Road today he quoted a line from an ancient Roman poet called Catullus. You'd never think of ancient Roman poets being romantic but this really was.

'Give me a thousand kisses, then a hundred, then another thousand,' quoted John in a very intense voice. And then he added. 'What's good enough for the Romans is good enough for me.' And then he kissed me. It was better than any labels, so what does Cass know?

Anyway, when we weren't talking about Latin poetry we were talking about LIFE. John says nothing could stop him from writing.

'Even if I was told I would have to live in poverty forever,' he said dramatically. 'Even if I had to live in a garret ...'

'What exactly is a garret?' I asked.

'An attic,' said John.

That doesn't sound so bad to me. Attics have nice slopey walls which I always think is very cute. Ellie's bedroom is an attic conversion and it's nicer than my room. Although maybe he doesn't mean an attic conversion but an actual attic, with a water tank and no windows? That would be fairly horrible. Still, I can't imagine why he would have to live in one. I mean, how would it come up? When is anyone going to say to him 'You must choose between living in an attic or never writing again?'

Anyway, I didn't say this to him. And he hadn't finished.

'Even if I had to lose my entire family,' he cried. 'Nothing could stop me from writing! If I had to choose between my parents' lives and my ability to write, I would have to choose writing! My own life wouldn't be worth living if I couldn't write!'

I don't think it's very likely that he will ever have to choose between any of these things, but it just shows how passionate he is about his work. Which is surely a good thing. I felt all exhilarated listening to him, like anything is possible. We have arranged to meet in town tomorrow and I can't wait.

I have to admit, though, that when I came home it was

quite a relief to just slump on the couch with my parents and watch a silly sitcom. It is very exciting being with John, but it is not very relaxing. Still, that's what home is for, isn't it?

SATURDAY ☺

John and I met in town today and went for black coffee (him) and hot chocolate (me). I told both Cass and Alice beforehand that we were meeting up and made it clear that I have not forgotten about them. I am sticking to my rules!

Alice and Richard are meeting in town today too, so I felt a bit bad about Cass being left on her own, but she said she was going to give Liz a ring and see if she wanted to look at guitars and instruments in music shops. So we were all happy.

It was a lovely afternoon. John brought a book of poetry by WB Yeats and when we went for a walk in Stephen's Green he stopped by the band stand and read one of them to me. It was about golden cloths and spreading dreams under your feet and him standing there reading it to me in the twilight was the most romantic thing that has ever happened to me. It was like something in a book or a film. It felt very grown up.

Of course, I was brought back to earth when I got home by my stupid parents. I knew I had to tell them about John because I knew if I didn't Rachel would eventually say something awful about him, so when I got home I told them I was seeing a boy from the musical called John Kowalski, and he was very nice. And I told them that that was all I was going to say about it so they needn't bother asking any questions thanks very much.

You'd think that would satisfy them, but no!

'Kowalski ...' said my mum thoughtfully. 'Is his dad's name Jan, by any chance?'

'I don't know,' I said. I mean, why would it come up?

'It's just when I went to the garden centre down the road the other week with Maria, we met a friend of hers called Jan Kowalski who has a son about your age,' she went on. 'We were talking to him for ages and he seemed very nice. He's Polish – he's lived here for years. He runs a community radio project and teaches media classes in a VEC out in west Dublin. His wife's Irish – I think she's a social worker. Does that ring any bells?'

'That can't be John's parents,' I said. 'He says they think of nothing but money and trivial things.'

'Ah,' said Mum. 'That doesn't sound like this couple. Maria told me he won some social entrepreneur award last year for all his good works.'

Anyway, Mum then got a bit patronising and said she was glad I'd met someone else after all my moping over Paperboy (that word again!), but then she said that boys weren't the most important thing in the world and I shouldn't think I needed a boyfriend to be happy. Obviously I know this, but I'm not going to turn down John just to prove it, am I?

MONDAY

It turns out that the Jan Kowalski Maria-from-round-the-corner knows is John's dad!

'Oh yeah,' he said, a bit reluctantly, when I asked him about it. 'That's him. He's obsessed with teaching idiots how to make radio programmes about local history and stuff. It's so boring.'

'But you said your parents were obsessed with money,' I said. 'I thought they'd be, like, greedy investment bankers who don't care about the world. Not people who do community work.'

'They are obsessed with money,' said John crossly. 'And trivial nonsense. They're always going on about stupid bills and stuff.'

I suppose if you are an artist like John then things like bills do seem trivial. Maybe he's right about Mum not being a proper artist; she certainly goes on about bills all the time.

TUESDAY ☾

I told Mrs Harrington a lie today. I said my parents were going to the show next Saturday instead of Friday. She looked so pleased after I told her that I felt a bit guilty, even though she is insane.

'I can't wait to meet your mammy at last!' she said. 'Do you think she'll mind if my husband and I bring a few books for her to sign?'

The thought of her bringing in a big stack of books for no reason made me feel even guiltier.

'Um, she mightn't have time,' I said. 'Why don't you bring them to me at school one at a time and I'll take them home and get her to sign them?'

I have no idea why I said that. I felt sorry for her at the time, being lied to by me, but now I'm going to have to cart home books for her. Possibly for weeks. Mum's written a lot of books and I'm pretty sure Mrs Harrington has every single one of them.

Anyway, I have got my own allocated tickets now. We cast members can only buy four tickets each. Mine are going to Mum, Dad, Rachel and Daisy. Yes, Rachel is such a noble sister that she is willing to sacrifice a Friday night out with her beloved Tom to see me on stage. At least, that's what she said. Frankly, I think turning up to see me perform is the least a sister can do. Jessie's sister, Kate, is coaching her every night and going through all her songs. But then, I suppose Kate is studying music in college. I don't think Rachel would be much good at coaching.

At least I don't have any little siblings. I do not understand small children these days; they're all mad. I can't believe I was like that when I was their age. Cass's brother Nick is bad enough, but that's nothing compared to my neighbours. When I was almost home from school I met Mrs Mulligan from across the road with the littlest Mulligan, the one who's always tormenting me with her stupid dancing.

'Hi there, Rebecca,' said Mrs Mulligan. 'How's the school musical going? Your mum told me about it.'

The little Mulligan didn't do anything; she just looked at me in a very innocent way. TOO INNOCENT.

'Pretty well, thanks,' I said. 'It's on next Friday.'

'Well, break a leg,' said Mrs Mulligan. 'Come on, Sorcha.'

And off they went. But when they had passed me, the kid looked back, made a ridiculous face, and gyrated at me in a taunting manner! And, of course, her mother didn't see a thing.

On the plus side, I suppose it proves that normal people can be closely related to enormous freaks. Mrs Mulligan and her husband always seem perfectly fine and look what they've produced. It's like me and my parents in reverse.

WEDNESDAY

John and I went outside to the bike racks during the break today. When we got there he put his arms around me. He is so tall. Under a lamp post next to the bike racks is not a very obvious romantic location, but, actually, it all felt very dramatic as the light shone down on us. It made John's eyes look very dark. His floppy fringe was sort of falling over his face and he pushed it back. And then he smiled at me.

'You know, Rafferty,' he said. 'I really feel like kissing you now.' And he did. Which was very nice. Then he took out a little grey book from his back pocket and read me a poem by a person called e.e.cummings who, as he pointed out afterwards, never used capital letters. Who knew you were allowed do that in proper poetry? It was a lovely poem, all about the rain and having small hands.

The thing is, I am not sure what to do when John reads poetry to me. In a way it is as romantic as it sounds because when he does it he sort of gazes into my eyes and looks very serious and dashing. But in another way I feel a bit awkward. What am I meant to do when he is gazing and reading and being serious? Should I just gaze back at him? Should I smile? Should I look very serious? And what do I do with my hands? I just sort of clasped them together in front of my chest this afternoon, but what if that looks like I am praying? That would be very weird. I had no idea big dramatic romance was so complicated. It never looks like this in films.

THURSDAY

I haven't mailed Paperboy and told him about John. I am not sure whether I should or not. I mean, would I want Paperboy to tell me if he was sort of seeing someone? I don't think I would. Even though we have officially moved on.

I talked about it to Cass and Alice at lunchtime today.

'Well, you don't want to lie to him, Bex,' said Alice.

'But it's not really lying to not say anything,' said Cass. 'Who owes who an e-mail at the moment?'

'Um, it's his turn to write to me,' I said.

'Well then,' said Cass. 'Wait until he writes back and, I dunno, take it from there.'

Even saintly Alice agreed this was probably the best plan. But I was still thinking about this evening so, very reluctantly, I went to talk to Rachel (when she finally got off the phone to Tom, the Boyfriend Who Can Do No Wrong).

'Hmm,' she said, when I had told her all. 'If he hadn't sent you that let's-move-on e-mail I would definitely say tell him. But to be honest if you both know you're not still going out, I think there's no point in making a big deal out of the whole thing. Just leave it and see what happens.'

I think they are all probably right. Which makes me feel better. The whole thing has made me, I dunno, properly accept that me and Paperboy are not going out anymore. Which is sad, but it is also okay.

And I do really like John. Every time I look across the

rehearsal room my stomach flips over. He always looks so serious and handsome when he's listening to Cathy, like he's really concentrating on something important. I am not sure I ever look so attractive during rehearsals. The other day I was concentrating very hard on what Ms Byrne was saying and Alice ended up waving her hands in front of my eyes because she thought I'd gone into some sort of trance.

'Your eyes kind of glazed over,' she said. Which is not a very attractive look at all, really.

FRIDAY ☺

Cass is being very noble this week. She keeps walking ahead of me after rehearsal so me and John can walk down the road on our own. She is truly a great friend.

'I do appreciate it, you know,' I said. I don't want her to think I am returning to my old self-obsessed ways.

'Meh, it's okay,' said Cass. 'I can listen to my iPod. It's actually quite nice, not having to listen to you for a while – I'm joking! Don't hit me!'

As if I would.

So John and I walked down Griffith Avenue together after

rehearsal. It is weird. He doesn't like holding hands when we walk down the road. He says it's a sign of bourgeois tradition. I am not sure what that means, but I think it has something to do with his strange fear of labels and stuff. But, anyway, I told him about the story and how maybe I should just give in and write something funny instead of a serious exploration of a young actress's life. 'Like, maybe I could just write something fun about a girl like me,' I said. 'What do you think?'

But John was not impressed.

'Rafferty,' he said. 'You're an intelligent girl. You're too intelligent to just waste your time on fluff like your mother.'

'Well, her books aren't actually funny ...' I began.

'It's all trivial nonsense!' said John. 'I really don't understand how smart people can read that sort of thing, let alone write it. Literature is meant to be about big ideas.' He turned to me. 'I know you can write something great if you really try. You don't need to write some cheap comedy.'

And then he kissed me.

It's weird, at the time it felt like he was saying something positive about me being great writer, but now I am not sure he is right. About me being able to write something great and serious, and about funny books in general. I mean, most of my favourite books are funny. I am reading an excellent funny book now called *The Pursuit of Love*, which is about very posh girls in the olden days. Not only does it make me laugh, but it is educating me about life in the past (for posh people)! What is wrong with funny books? Why shouldn't I write them if I want to?

But I know he meant well. And surely it is good that he has faith in my literary powers. Anyway, I will see him all day tomorrow at the big weekend rehearsal. The live band – who are all friends of Cathy, apparently – are coming to run through the songs with us. Alice suggested that a bunch of us go out for coffee after the rehearsal, but I can't because my parents have organised yet another weekend outing. And this time it is not even to someone I like; it's to my awful aunt Celine, Dad's sister, the one who likes to poke at me and Rachel and tell us how scrawny we are. She is always being rude about what people look like. I know if we were larger she'd poke at us and tell us how fat we were – I've seen her do it to my cousin Katie. She has no manners.

My mum absolutely hates it when Celine does this. Every time Celine says something about us or our cousins, my mum says that Rachel/me/whichever cousin is Celine's latest victim 'looks perfectly fine and absolutely lovely' in a very firm voice. And as soon as we leave the house, she always says, 'Just ignore Celine, girls, she means well.'

I bet she doesn't. She's just a rude cow, but Mum has to say this to be polite. Dad doesn't get along with Celine either, but we have to go tomorrow because it's her birthday. It's so unfair.

SATURDAY ☺

Today something that I've been dreading happened. Mum and Dad met John.

It happened like this. We had our super-long Saturday rehearsal with the live band, which went pretty well, actually. Although Sam tripped over something on his way on to the 'stage'. He was covered in ink, too, like a pen had leaked all over his hands. He really is a bit of a klutz. John is the opposite. He looks so debonair on stage. When I met him during the break I said, 'Hello, Mr Banks.'

He raised an eyebrow. 'Well, hello, random member of the chorus.' Then he grinned. 'It's really coming together out there, isn't it? I mean, for a school musical. It's all such good stage experience.'

'As long as Sam doesn't fall over anything,' I said.

'Oh, he's alright,' said John. 'At least I don't share any scenes with him, so I don't have to worry about him falling over me. My bits should all be fine.'

Afterwards my parents were collecting me to go to Celine's stupid birthday party. I had told them to wait in the car and park far away from the school gates, so John wouldn't pass them on his way home, but, of course, they ignored my instructions. Instead, when we walked up the school drive they were both STANDING THERE AT THE GATE SMIRKING AT ME. Oh, the horror. I hate them.

'Hi, Rebecca!' called my mother.

'Hi, love!' said my dad cheerily.

The shame.

And, of course, I couldn't ignore them. And I couldn't ignore John.

'Oh, hi,' I said grumpily.

'Hi there,' said my mother, beaming at John like a psychopath. 'You must be John. I'm Rebecca's mother, Rosie.'

'Oh,' said John, looking slightly freaked out. 'Um, yes. Hello.'

And he shook hands with both my parents like a proper grown-up and started to look like his usual confident self again.

'So John,' said my dad. 'I hear you're a writer.'

Oh God, why did he have to say that? It looked like I'd been talking about him to my parents. Which I had, but only because they made me.

'Yes,' said my mum brightly. 'Like me!'

'Well,' said John, and he smiled. 'Not quite like you. I write pretty serious stuff.'

'Ah,' said my mother. She was still smiling, but there was a glint in her eye. 'I see. What sort of things do you write about?'

'Oh, you know,' said John. 'I write about real life. Real issues. War. Love. Death. Adventure. Philosophy. Escaping conformity. Not, you know, romantic fluff.'

'Wow,' said my mother. 'I'm impressed.'

'Yeah,' said John. He looked very seriously at my mum. 'I couldn't write the sort of light entertainments that you write.'

'I bet you couldn't,' said Mum.

'I'm working on some theatre pieces at the moment,' said John.

'Very impressive,' said Dad politely.

'So,' I said desperately. 'Don't we have to go? Aren't we late for Celine?'

'Ah,' said my dad. 'I suppose we are. Nice to meet you, John. Good luck with the musical – Rosie and I were in a musical ourselves once so we can't wait to see it!'

For a terrible second I thought he and Mum were going to go on about *The Pirates of Penzance* for the ten millionth time which would have sent John running for the hills, but luckily they didn't.

'Yes, I'm sure it'll be brilliant,' said my mum. 'Keep up the good writing work!'

'I'll try,' said John, and smiled at them very politely. He looked at me and grinned. 'Bye, Rebecca.'

And I had to go. Obviously there would be no kissing goodbye in front of my parents. When we were in the car (Rachel had waited there because she, unlike SOME PEOPLE, know that most people do not want to come out of a rehearsal with their sort-of boyfriend and find their entire family waiting for them) Mum said, 'Well, he seems like a ... very serious boy. He cares about his writing.'

'Of course he does,' I said. 'He's a proper artist.'

'Hmmm,' said my mum. And then she started arguing with my dad about the best route to Celine's house.

On the plus side Celine wasn't as irritating as usual. She

had a terrible cold so she couldn't say very much and we didn't have to stay long. And when we got home my parents got another posh take-away to cheer us up after the visit. So the day wasn't a total disaster. But still, I wish my stupid parents hadn't turned up. I bet John thought they were enormous freaks. Which they are.

SUNDAY

Oh my God. Just when I thought my parents had run out of new ways to embarrass me, they come up with a new one. As if yesterday wasn't bad enough, today we were having dinner and Mum and Dad started going on about *The Pirates of Penzance* yet again. And then Mum said, 'You know what, Ed? I'd really like to do it again.'

Rachel and I looked at each other.

'Mum,' said Rachel patiently. 'You can't just put on your 1985 production of *The Pirates of Penzance* on your own. That's insane. And I can't imagine all your old castmates would want to do it anyway.'

Mum looked at her. 'I don't mean put on the Pirates again,' she said. 'Of course that's a mad idea. Not least because nothing could ever capture the excitement of that particular production. No, I mean your dad and I could join a musical society. There's one in Glasnevin as far as I know. We should check it out.'

I hoped Dad would say, 'What a ridiculous idea, Rosie, you must have gone mad.' But he didn't. He looked delighted.

'That's a great idea!' he said. 'I'll go and look it up online after dinner.'

And he did. And it turns out that not only is there indeed a local musical society, but they are holding auditions for their next production in about six weeks. My crazy parents are counting the days.

'I'll have to dig out my tap shoes,' said my dad. 'I bet they're up in the attic somewhere.'

'You have TAP SHOES?' said Rachel in horror.

'Of course,' said Dad. 'I did all sorts of dancing in the Pirates. Jazz ballet, tap, disco. I've told you, it really was an imaginative production.'

The mind reels. Luckily, Rachel is just as appalled by the idea of our parents prancing around on stage again as I am.

'Our only hope,' she said later, when we were loading the dishwasher like the servants we are, and our parents were relaxing in the sitting room, 'is that it's almost two months until that audition. Maybe they'll forget about it by then.'

'I wouldn't count on it,' I said. And I wouldn't. I know my mental parents. Once they get an idea into their heads, there's no stopping them.

I can't tell John about it. I have a feeling he thinks my parents are trivial fools anyway. And this would only prove him right. We met up this afternoon and went for a walk around Griffith Avenue. John started talking about life experience and how important it is to LIVE before you write.

'I want to experience everything, Rafferty,' he said. 'I want to live, and laugh, and love!'

Heavens.

Anyway, that gave me the chance to ask something I'd been wondering about. I remembered Bike Boy saying it was ages since John had broken up with his last girlfriend – or sort-of-girlfriend – ages ago, but John had never said anything about it himself.

'So,' I said. 'Have you ever ... have you ever, like, gone out with a girl? Before me?'

'You know I don't like to be pinned down, Rafferty,' he said. 'But yeah, I was with a girl called Lucy last summer. I met her at a poetry workshop thing. She was pretty talented, actually.'

I instantly hated this Lucy.

'What happened?' I said, even though I wasn't sure I really wanted to know.

'She just didn't understand me,' said John. 'She didn't get my writing. She was more interested in her own stuff. Not like you, Rafferty. You know how important it is to me.'

Ooh.

I thought he was going to ask me about my romantic history, such as it is, but he didn't. But I thought I should bring it up, so I said, 'I was seeing someone last year too.' I was going to say that I met him because of his Paperboy role, but somehow I didn't want to. It felt like, I dunno, too personal. So I said, 'We got together after I was in the Battle of the Bands.'

'Oh yeah, your band,' said John. 'You know, I was thinking about what I said the other week, and I really think you should try and learn the guitar. Or at least the bass. I mean, you don't really want to be stuck back there behind the others, sweating away on the drums, do you? It's not very dignified, is it? It's not very, I dunno, ladylike.'

I didn't know what to say. I mean, I don't want to look like a total hobo, but I would always rather have fun and do something cool than be ladylike. So eventually I said, 'I don't really care about being elegant on stage. I mean, I'd rather play the drums.'

And John laughed and kissed the top of my head and said, 'You really are one of a kind.'

I have to admit this really annoyed me. Like me caring about my drums was just some sort of silly quirky thing. But before I could do anything about it, I got a text from my dad telling me I was half an hour late and I had to come home for dinner, so I just had time to say goodbye and trot up Gracepark Road at top speed (oh, John is such a good kisser). And now a few hours have gone by I've thought about it and I realise that John just doesn't understand my love of drumming because he's never actually seen me do it. Once the band is back together and he can see how much I love it, I'm sure he'll come round and realise how awesome it is. Paperboy thought it was great that I played the drums. I am sure John will too.

MONDAY

Mrs Harrington brought in the first of her Rosie Carberry collection today. It is a giant hardback and it weighs a ton. I might have known she'd have all the first editions.

'Can you get your mammy to sign it "To Patricia and Gerard"?' said Mrs Harrington. 'And I'll bring another one in tomorrow!'

Oh God, I'm going to be carrying giant books to and from school for weeks. AND when she turns up on Saturday she's going to find out that I lied about Mum and Dad going that night. What have I let myself in for?

That is not the only thing I feel slightly guilty about. After rehearsal today, I was about to tell Cass and Alice I was leaving with John when he said, 'Oh, come on, Rafferty, we'll be here all night if you have to find both of them, and we hardly get to spend any time together as it is! You don't have to tell your friends about your every move!'

'Oh,' I said. 'I suppose not.'

'So let's just go,' he said. 'They won't mind. I mean, Cass is off backstage somewhere and Alice seems, you know, otherwise engaged with Richard.'

So off we went.

'You know, Rafferty, you worry too much about other people,' said John. 'You need to put yourself first sometimes! It's the only way to get what you want. You can't be a doormat.'

I know he is right. My problem is that I am meant to be actively trying to be nicer and not a selfish beast. Surely there must be some sort of mid-point between being a doormat and being, you know, nice and thoughtful? Anyway, I clearly haven't found it because I feel a bit guilty now. I texted Alice and Cass to say sorry and they both said it was fine, but still. Leaving Cass to walk alone is one thing as long as we're both, like, aware of it, but sneaking off seems a bit wrong.

It was lovely walking with John, though. We talked about books we loved.

John urged me to read Jack Kerouac. 'It's written in what he called spontaneous prose,' he said. 'Like a stream of consciousness, everything just tumbling out. It's really intense. You have to read it. He's like, playing with language.'

'I'm reading a great book too,' I said. '*The Pursuit of Love*. It's by a woman called Nancy Mitford and it's all about these posh sisters and their cousin and they end up, like, being in wars and stuff, but it's really funny and ...'

'There's nothing funny in *On the Road*,' said John sternly. 'It's all about passion and life. And the need to just, like, get in a car and drive across America.'

'Well, there's some travel in *The Pursuit of Love*,' I said. 'The main character ends up going to ...'

But John was so caught up in his love for *On the Road*, he didn't seem to notice I'd said anything.

'I'd love to do that this summer,' he said. 'Just go to America and hit the road like Sal Paradise and Dean Moriarty.'

'Wow, can you drive?' I said. 'I didn't think you could get a licence until you were eighteen.'

'Well, I can't actually drive yet,' said John. 'But I'll be sixteen in July. I could do the test in America. I heard you just have to, like, start the car properly and you pass your test over there.'

'Wow, that would be cool. But how will you pay for it?' I said.

'Oh, Rafferty, all these questions!' said John. 'I'll always find a way to do what I want.'

I bet he will too; he is so determined. I wouldn't know where to start if I wanted to fund a drive across America. I only have a hundred euro in my savings account and I have to ask my tyrannical parents for permission to take any of it out.

TUESDAY ☾

We have rehearsals every day this week because the musical is on Friday. All the other teachers are getting pretty cross. Miss

Kelly, unsurprisingly, is the worst.

'I want all of you in this room giving me your full attention on Monday when this nonsense is over,' she said grimly. 'There'll be no more excuses for lazily done homework and girls staring out the window thinking about dance steps instead of concentrating on serious geography issues. I might even give you a test.'

We all stared at her in horror. Kelly's tests are terrifying. Not least because they are generally about what terrible environmental disaster is most likely to afflict various parts of the world. Jessie had nightmares about nuclear power stations and earthquakes after the last one.

Anyway, Kelly relented by the end of the class and said she wasn't going to give us a test.

'At least, I won't give you a test next week,' she added. 'But maybe the week after that. So I want you all back working very, very hard on Monday.'

I can't really imagine what it'll be like when the musical is over. It feels like it's been our entire universe for the past couple of months. I can't believe it's only a few weeks since we were all standing around a piano going through those songs for the first time. We know them all backwards now.

I still felt bad about deserting Cass and Alice after rehearsal yesterday, so when today's rehearsal was over I told John I wanted to wait for Cass so we could all walk together. He rolled his eyes but said, 'If you insist, Rafferty.'

Cass seemed faintly surprised but pleased when she saw me waiting for her and we all strolled out together. She was covered in paint from some last-minute set-painting.

'It's all coming together now,' she said. 'Did you see the carousel?'

'Yeah, it looks great!' I said.

'A bit garish, though,' said John. 'I wish we could have a more, you know, experimental set. Like, instead of an actual carousel, there could just be some giant white spheres in a circle.'

Cass looked at him. 'I don't think Richard and Vanessa would be very comfortable trying to sit on giant white spheres,' she said.

'It was just an idea,' said John loftily. 'I suppose I'll have to think more about that sort of thing when I'm studying drama.'

'Oh, you want to do drama in college?' said Cass. 'Cool.'

'Well, yeah, of course I do,' said John. 'I've always known exactly what I want to do when I leave school.'

'But you've got another two years before you have to think of college,' said Cass. 'I mean, maybe you'll decide that it's better to do, I dunno, another arts degree and read loads of stuff and then become a director. Or you could even become something else.'

John looked appalled. 'I'm not going to waste time on anything like that! I've got a vision!'

'But, I mean, you're sort of pinning yourself down, aren't you?' said Cass. 'You should leave your options open!'

'I don't need to,' said John.

'Don't you want to be a set designer, Cass?' I said, trying to smooth things over. 'That's a vision!'

'Oh yeah,' said Cass. 'But I'm not sure how I'll end up there at the moment. I mean, I might go to college and find something else I like and do something totally different. Or I might apply to, I dunno, set designing and not get in and then have to think of something else.'

'I'm going to get in to drama college,' said John, but he looked very annoyed. 'Not everyone wants to faff around waiting to find out what they like.'

'Fair enough, I suppose not,' said Cass. She didn't seem bothered, but somehow John seemed more sulky than usual.

I was kind of relieved when we reached the corner of Griffith Avenue and she walked on home while I stayed to say goodbye to John.

'God, I thought she'd never go,' said John, which was a bit unfair because as soon as we reached the corner she'd said, 'See you tomorrow!' and left. 'I know she's one of your best friends but God, she's so argumentative!'

'Oh, she's not really,' I said. 'She just disagreed with you! And she was very nice about it. It wasn't a big deal.'

'Maybe not,' said John. He smiled at me. 'I suppose it's because I just wanted to be on my own with you so I could do this.'

And then he kissed me. I wish Cass knew how sweet he can be when it's just the two of us.

WEDNESDAY

Alice is getting a bit nervous about Friday. Not because of the show itself – at least not just because of the show. But because her parents will meet Bike Boy for the first time.

'Why are you so worried, Alice?' said Cass. 'I mean, it's not like Richard is really rude or obnoxious or anything. He'll be fine! They'll love him!'

'But what if they decide he's not, like, worthy of their family or something?' said Alice.

'Alice,' said Cass. 'You are not living in Victorian times. They're not trying to marry you off to a lord. Plus you and Richard have, you know, basic social skills – well, he does anyway. I'm starting to wonder about you. And your parents are pretty normal as far as parents go.'

'Apart from liking my mum's books, but that won't affect them with Richard,' I said.

'True,' said Cass. 'So yeah, I'm sure the meet-up will go okay.' She turned to me. 'It was fine when Paperboy met your parents, wasn't it?'

'Oh yeah,' I said. 'They only met him a couple of times but they loved him.'

'And that was after your mum had caught you snogging outside the Knitting Factory after the Battle of the Bands!' said Cass. 'But even that didn't prejudice her against him. And what about John, didn't they meet him on Saturday?'

'Oh yeah,' I said. 'Um, that was fine too.'

This seemed to comfort Alice a bit. Actually, the whole thing got me wondering about meeting John's parents. On the way home from rehearsal today I asked what night they were coming.

'They're not,' he said. 'Coming, that is.'

'Really?' I said. 'That's a shame. Why can't they come?'

'I told them not to,' he said. 'How can I concentrate on my art when I know those two idiots are in the audience cheering and clapping? It would be a distraction.'

'But don't they want to come?' I said.

'Oh, they want to come all right,' said John. 'But I said that if they came, it would totally wreck my performance, and did they want that on their consciences? Also, they'd have to buy their tickets through me, and I won't get them for them. So they're not coming.'

I felt a bit sorry for John's parents. But, on the other hand, I can understand where he's coming from. I kind of wish my own parents weren't coming. It will only fuel their musical obsession. The only bad thing about this school musical is that it triggered my parents' memories of their supposed glory days. I never want to hear the words Pirates of Penzance again.

THURSDAY

Show tomorrow! We had a dress rehearsal this evening with the band, and tomorrow all us musical people have the morning off, then we have one last run-through in the afternoon and a few hours off before going back for the actual show.

Vanessa is going to spend tomorrow morning getting a blow dry from some ridiculously posh salon in town.

'I have to look my best,' she says, even though she's going to be wearing a hat for the entire show. She's as mad as ever. She's still convinced that the *Irish Times* are going to send a critic. She was going on about this today, so I tried to tell her that my mum has lots of friends who are journalists and they do not review school shows, but she doesn't care.

'You don't understand, Rebecca,' she said snootily. 'I've sent all the arts writers invitations. I got them printed up specially.'

I didn't bother telling her this wouldn't make any difference. From the way she carries on you'd think we were going on stage in the Abbey, not appearing in the St Dominic's school hall on a stage that usually doubles as the music room. I was going to write that she'll get a terrible shock when she realises there isn't, like, a giant press section but if the last few months have taught me anything it's that nothing shocks or bothers Vanessa for long. She always lands on her feet. Even though she doesn't deserve it. I'm just not going to tell her about Daisy coming. There's no way she'll believe a critic is coming just because she's my godmother.

I didn't see John properly after the rehearsal today because it's his dad's birthday so he had to rush off and get a bus to town for the birthday dinner. His parents thought it would be good for him to go out the night before the performance rather than sitting at home brooding about it, but he didn't want to go at all. It's in some posh restaurant, which he didn't approve of.

'I can't believe I'm going to have to spend, like, two hours in that tacky hell hole, surrounded by fawning waiters,' he said gloomily. 'Restaurants like that are just temples to greed! And my parents keep acting like it's such a great treat for me.' He put on a silly voice. '"Oh John, it'll be so relaxing for you on the night before the show!" They're always fussing over me; it's tormenting me.'

'You could protest,' I suggested. 'Only eat bread and drink water. Or eat nothing! '

'Well, I don't know' said John slowly. 'I feel I can challenge the system more by ostentatiously eating as much as possible.'

I am not sure exactly what he means by this. I have a feeling he is just going to eat a lot. I have to admit that John's parents don't actually sound that bad. Much less embarrassing than mine. His only real problem seems to be that they're too nice to him. Still, I suppose they don't understand his artistic temperament.

Actually, I was glad I got to just amble down the road with Cass, messing about like in the olden days. John is very exciting, but all those intense conversations can be a bit exhausting, especially when I'm all worked up about the show tomorrow. Cass and I spent the walk doing impersonations of various teachers singing the songs from *Mary Poppins*. I think my version of Miss Kelly doing 'Let's Go Fly a Kite' was pretty good, but Cass's portrayal of Mrs Harrington singing 'A Spoonful of Sugar' was even better. She got the facial expressions just right. Anyway, I can't remember when I laughed so much. It was quite nice to be all trivial again.

I can't believe what happened today. I am in a rage. I hate John Kowalski!

Well, maybe I don't entirely hate him. But I am very, very angry with him. He is a stupid selfish baby and he's wrecked the entire musical.

What happened is this. We met up as planned this morning and walked down to the café place for breakfast. He still didn't hold my hand on the way, but to be honest, I don't care now because I don't want my hand held by a TRAITOR. Which he is.

Anyway, we got there and ordered our breakfasts and then he took a deep breath and said, 'Rafferty, I have something to tell you.'

Of course, I immediately felt sick because I thought he was going to break up with me. Or tell me he had a secret other girlfriend. Oh God, maybe he was secretly having an affair with Vanessa. I mean, I know I'd been a bit annoyed with him, but I didn't want him running off with someone else. But he didn't do either of those things.

'You know that short play? That got into the final? Well, there's going to be an awards ceremony in Cork and they've asked me to go,' he said.

I felt relief wash over me. He wasn't breaking up with me! Or going out with Vanessa!

'Wow, that's brilliant,' I said, in a very enthusiastic voice. Because I am a very good sort-of-girlfriend. Or I WAS.

'Yeah,' said John. 'The thing is, there was a mix-up with the invitation and I should have been told about the ceremony when they told me I was on the shortlist. It turns out it's on tonight.'

'Oh,' I said. Then it struck me what meant. 'Oh, no, you'll miss it! Oh, that's awful. But if you win they'll send up your trophy and whatever, won't they?'

'Well, they won't have to,' said John. 'I mean, I'm going down to the ceremony. I've already bought my train ticket. My aunt and uncle live in Cork so I can stay with them. I can't miss this!' He kind of laughed, like he knew I would agree with him. But of course I didn't. I just stared at him like a loon. I couldn't believe what he was saying.

'But ... the musical,' I spluttered. 'You can't miss the musical!'

But he just laughed. Laughed! Like it wasn't a big deal!

'Oh come on, Rafferty,' he said. 'It's just a silly secondary school show. It's kids' stuff. It's *Mary Poppins*, for God's sake! You can't seriously think I'd put that over a prestigious writing award ceremony, do you?'

'Yes!' I said. 'I do! Because loads and loads of people have been slaving away at it for weeks and weeks! And if you drop out, it'll be wrecked! You don't have an understudy!'

'Oh, they can get Sam to read my lines from a script,' said John dismissively. 'He can pick up the songs easily enough. We don't have any scenes together. It's not a big deal.'

I was so angry, I was nearly shaking.

'It's a huge deal!' I cried. 'Sam is far too nervous to do it properly! He's so clumsy! He was covered in ink on Saturday! We've worked so hard on this, and now you're going to wreck it! And at the last minute, too!'

'God, Rafferty, I thought you'd understand,' said John. He looked absolutely sullen. A tiny part of me thought how good-looking he was when he was all serious, but most of me was on fire with rage. I am sure I looked absolutely hideous because unlike John, who looks even more attractive when he is annoyed, I always go bright red in the face whenever I get angry. I will never have a moment like in a film where people are arguing and it's all sexy. But I don't care. You can't bother about what you look like all the time.

'What I do understand,' I said, 'is that you just put yourself first and you don't care about how anyone else feels!'

And as I said it I realised it was true. Not just about the

musical, but other things too. Like when he criticised my mum's books to me. Or when he didn't listen when I was talking about books I like. Or when he told me not to bother telling Cass and Alice when we were leaving. He has ALWAYS been a big selfish, cigarette-stinking baby and I just didn't want to notice it. But I do now. It was like a lightbulb going on inside me.

'Oh for God's sake, Rafferty, don't be so bloody childish,' said John. He didn't even sound that angry now. He sounded bored.

'I'm not being childish!' I hissed. 'You're the one who's ... shirking his responsibility! What about all the work all of us have put in? Cathy! Ms Byrne! Even Vanessa! We've been doing this for weeks and now you're going to drop out because you've found something better to do!'

'I can't believe you're having a bloody tantrum about this,' said John. 'I'm a writer. An artist. I'd do anything for my art. I thought you understood that. But you're acting just like my parents. They gave me a big lecture this morning about this rubbish too. They were acting like doing this stupid show was more important than my literary career.'

'Well, maybe they were right. Doing anything for your art shouldn't mean letting everyone else down,' I said. All of a sudden I knew I was going to burst into tears of rage so I got up and grabbed my coat and bag.

'I'm going home,' I said. 'And I never want to see you again, you selfish smelly beast.'

And I marched out. I was in a sort of rage trance. It was like a red mist had descended over my eyes. I barely knew where I was going until I arrived at my front door a few minutes ago.

So basically, I have to go to school in an hour and do the last rehearsal even though the musical is wrecked. I don't care if John is a great artist or not. Decent human beings don't let other people down. They don't basically wreck something loads of other people have worked hard on just so they can go off to Cork and MAYBE get a prize for some stupid play. I know his writing is important, but so is the musical! So are all of us! And now all our practising will go to waste because the best we can do for one of the lead parts is Sam shuffling around the stage with a script in his hand trying to sing 'Let's Go Fly a Kite'. The whole show will be a disaster. I mean, there's just one rehearsal left, and it's not like there's anyone else who knows how to play Mr Banks properly.

Oh my God. I have an idea. An amazing idea. Maybe the musical is not wrecked after all.

I am going to ring Jane. I just hope she takes her phone to school and puts it on at morning break.

LATER

Jane is a heroine!

She has saved the show. Well, I hope she's saved the show. I mean, she could, like, fall off the stage tonight and wreck everything, but she's been doing this sort of thing for years so I think she'll be okay. I rang her and THANK GOD she had her phone on during break even though no one's meant to have their phone on at school, and I told her about evil stinky John.

'I know it's a while since you were Mr Banks,' I said. 'But is there any way you could step in? We've got one last rehearsal this afternoon, but I know you get a half-day on Fridays ...'

'Wow,' said Jane. 'It's very short notice. But of course I'll help. Imagine him leaving you all in the lurch at the last minute! What a fool.'

I told you she was a heroine (she is also right about John being a fool). I told her I'd meet her at my school gates at two for the run through.

Cass and Alice were very surprised to see me walk into the hall with Jane. But they were even more surprised when I told them about John being an evil selfish traitor. Even Alice, who never gets panicky, went a bit wobbly.

'Are you sure you want to do it, Jane?' she said.

'Oh, totally sure,' said Jane. 'I mean, it's not like I'm not used to performing with Vanessa. And Mr Banks is sort of Mary Poppins's enemy for most of it, so that'll be fun.'

I didn't catch John's eye when he turned up. In fairness to him he didn't faff around. He went straight up to Cathy and Ms Byrne, who had just walked in, and a minute later I heard Cathy say, 'Oh my God, John, I don't believe this. It's incredibly unprofessional!'

Ha! I have to admit it was great hearing a grown-up tell him that he wasn't acting like a sophisticated great artist after all. Anyway, John looked a bit ashamed for a second, but then he sort of tossed his hair back and said, loud enough for us to hear, 'I'm sorry, Cathy, but my writing will always come first.' And then he stalked out of the room. I have to admit that he did look very moody and dramatic. But that is not enough for me now.

Anyway, everyone realised what was going on and the whole room went mental. Everyone was totally freaking out.

'Sam, come here,' said Ms Byrne in a very harassed way. 'You're going to have to do Mr Banks.'

'But I don't know half the words!' said poor Sam, who had gone white with fear. 'More than half!'

'Well, you'll just have to carry a script,' said Ms Byrne. 'Now then ...'

'Um, Ms Byrne?' I said. Well, actually, I had to kind of shriek to be heard over the din because of everyone going a bit mad. 'There's someone else who can do it.'

'Miss Rafferty, please don't say you can do it because you can't. At least Sam's been taking part in the principals' rehearsals.'

I was very annoyed by this, but because I have become so noble as a result of sticking to my rules I didn't say anything about it. I just said, 'No, here's my friend Jane Park. She's in a music and drama class and she played Mr Banks in her school musical last year.'

'Hello!' said Jane, and gave Ms Byrne a cheery wave.

Ms Byrne froze. So did most people in the hall. Things got very quiet.

'Come here,' she said. Jane went.

'Do you really know all the lines?' said Ms Byrne.

'Well, I'm a bit rusty, but more or less,' said Jane. 'I'll have a quick look over the script, but I know they'll come back to me.'

'Sing a few bars of, um, "Let's Go Fly A Kite",' said Ms Byrne.

She did. Beautifully. And in a voice that was boomy and manly but not ridiculous (in the manner of me booming in chorus rehearsals). It just shows what a good performer she is because she has quite a high voice normally.

Ms Byrne breathed a sigh of relief.

'Right,' she said. 'You'll do. Thank you very much indeed.'

'But what about the costume?' said Jane.

Ms Byrne looked a bit worried. But before she could say anything a very grand voice rang out from the stage.

'Do you really think I can't alter that traitorous boy's costume to fit this lovely young girl?' cried Mrs Limond. I knew she was okay really. 'Come here, child, and I'll take your measurements. Eleanor, I urgently need your assistance!'

And Ellie immediately leapt out from the side of the stage, holding a tape measure and a pair of scissors. I suppose Mrs Limond using her as a slave has turned out to be quite useful.

Once Jane had been measured and Ellie and Mrs Limond had gone off to their scissors and sewing machines, we went through the show. Obviously Jane was a bit rusty when she came to the lines, but the more we went through them the better she got. And most of the cast were so relieved that the show was going ahead, I think they were better than ever. Even Karen didn't annoy me too much.

The only problem was Vanessa. I think John's walkout actually freaked her out. She realised that him being gone could damage the show which meant her own chance at stardom. She hesitated a few times and once she dropped her special Mary Poppins's umbrella (it didn't break, thank goodness. I think Cass would have hit her with it if it had; she'd spent ages working on it). But she wasn't, like, a total disaster. Anyway, we've done our best. And in about two hours we'll be up on that stage and the show will go on.

Despite John Kowalski. Everyone is so annoyed with him. You should have heard Cass and Alice.

'He was never good enough for you, Bex!' cried Alice.

'He's not good enough for ... for ... a toad,' said Cass. 'That came out wrong, Bex. I didn't mean to compare you to a toad. But he's a fool!'

A part of me thought, well, if you thought he was so bad you could have told me, but mostly I thought, well, fair enough. I wouldn't really have listened to them if they had told me what they thought.

It's funny, you'd think I'd be heartbroken about him being a selfish babyhead, but I'm not. It's not like when Paperboy went or when I slowly realised he really wasn't coming back. I don't really know how I feel but I think it could be ...

Relief?

Right, I'm off to the school now. Wish me luck ...

SATURDAY ☺

WE ARE A HIT!

I can't believe it. We pulled it off.

Jane was fantastic! You would never have guessed when she strode out on the stage last night that she had only had one rehearsal. She was a born star. And she had a magical effect on everyone else. It was like we all realised she was going to pull it off and so everyone was full of enthusiasm and did their very, very best. Cathy didn't even have to do her scary evil-eye-glare at anyone. Alice and I sing-acted with all our might, but we made sure we didn't go over the top. And, in fairness to Vanessa, she really pulled it out of the bag. I had my doubts yesterday, but she was really, really good. I actually believed she was lovely, clever Mary Poppins which just shows what a good actor she is. But the real surprise of the show was Sam. He'd seemed so nervous at rehearsals, but once he was on stage he was absolutely amazing – really funny and confident. The audience gave a huge round of applause after his big scene. There must have been something in the air! Or maybe he was always that good and I didn't notice because I was gazing at John.

I think we all knew by the interval that it was going well. There was a real buzz in the room. And when we sang the last notes of the last song there was a huge, huge round of applause. Cathy and Ms Byrne were thrilled.

'You did it, girls and boys!' cried Cathy. 'You took that audience on a journey into the heart of *Mary Poppins* and they loved it! Bravo! Bravo!'

'You were great,' said Ms Byrne. But she was smiling, for once. 'Especially you, chorus. Excellent sing-acting.' And she looked at me and Alice and winked!

Mrs Limond was marching around backstage, waving a cigarette in a long holder. No one dared tell her not to smoke indoors, even though there were so many flammable fabrics in our costumes that if she'd waved the cigarette the wrong way we'd have all gone up in flames.

'A triumph, my dears, an absolute triumph,' she said. And then, to all our surprise, not least Ellie's, she looked at Ellie and said, 'Especially you, Eleanor. You did an excellent job. Thank you very much.'

So she must really have appreciated Ellie being her slave after all. Even though she never did figure out her real name.

The audience really seemed to enjoy the show. When we were actually on stage under the bright lights it was quite hard to see everyone out there, like when we played the Battle of the Bands, but I was still able to see none other than Bernard the Fairytale Prince right up in the front row. I almost felt bad for wondering if Karen had been making up their crazy relationship because he certainly does seem devoted. I was watching from the wings and he stood up and applauded like mad when she and Wiktoria did their song about wanting a nanny. In fact, at the end he even threw a bouquet of roses up on the stage for her! She went bright red and then beamed back at him and she looked so properly happy and not sneery that for a minute I didn't even hate her.

Also, I noticed Alison and Caroline were there too, but they were applauding normally like ordinary people, not devoted worshipers. And they didn't stand up like Bernard the Fairytale Prince did. Not even at the very end, when quite a few people stood up. I think Caroline and Alison might really have discovered their independence. There is no going back for them now.

Mum and Dad seemed to enjoy the show too, though not enough to throw giant bouquets at their daughter. And so did Daisy.

'You were brilliant, Bex,' said Dad. 'Even better than our *Pirates of Penzance.*'

Which, coming from him, was praise indeed.

'You really were' said Mum. 'All of you. That was some excellent acting during "Feed the Birds" from you and Alice.'

'We've been practising for ages,' I said modestly.

'You were great,' said Daisy. She laughed. 'I'll have to write that review for the *Times* now!' she joked.

'I KNEW IT,' said a crazed voice.

It was Vanessa! I hadn't noticed she was nearby. She practically grabbed Daisy, who was so stunned she just froze.

'Did you get my invitation?' said Vanessa.

'Oh,' said Daisy. 'Um, yes, the paper sent it on to me, but that's not why ...'

But before she had finished the sentence, Vanessa cried, 'I knew you'd come! I can't wait to see what you write about us!' She batted her eyelashes again. I don't know how she does it. 'Please, be kind. I'll look out for your review.' And she strutted off to the tea and biscuits.

She can look all she likes, there's never going to be a review. I hope she doesn't start harassing poor Daisy about it. I think Daisy was worried as well.

'She does know I was joking when I told you I'd write the review, doesn't she?' she said nervously.

'Oh, I'm sure she does,' I said, but I was only saying it to cheer her up. I bet Vanessa will be going through the paper for days, waiting for her write-up. It is actually quite a comfort to know that she is doomed to disappointment. Alice's parents weren't disappointed with Bike Boy, though. He totally charmed them. He even said 'Guten Abend!' to Alice's mother (Alice said later that this is practically all the German he knows, but it shows his good intentions and Alice's mother loved it), and her parents told him he should call out to their house next week so Alice needn't have worried at all.

Anyway, eventually I went home with my parents in a sort of daze. I thought I'd be too excited to sleep, but actually I was so exhausted by all the madness I fell asleep straight away. But now it's all a bit weird. When I woke up this morning I forgot what had happened for a second and then I remembered everything: John letting everyone down and then Jane saving the day and the show going well. I've been waiting to feel all heartbroken about the John thing, but it hasn't happened.

Instead, now I keep remembering more stuff, like the way he told me to learn the guitar because drums weren't girly enough. And how he acted like Cass had been picking a fight just because she disagreed with him. And how he told me I shouldn't write funny stories because they weren't proper books. And all the 'ooh, we can't label our relationship' stuff.

Oh my God, my phone is ringing. It's him.

LATER

Well, if I had any doubt that I did the right thing marching out yesterday I don't anymore. I almost didn't answer the phone, but I knew I had to talk to him eventually so I did.

'Rafferty!' he said. 'I came second! Which isn't quite as well as I hoped, obviously, but I was the youngest winner and the judge said I was really promising. You do understand why I had to go down there, don't you?'

Unbelievable!

'No, actually, I don't,' I said crossly.

'Oh, come on,' he said, sounding cross too. 'I was just going to tell you I forgive you for stomping off yesterday morning because I know it was a shock, but if you're going to act like a child ...'

'I'm not acting like a child,' I said. 'I'm acting like someone who's tired because they were in a show last night. Which went brilliantly, by the way, no thanks to you. Thanks for NOT ASKING ABOUT IT, THOUGH.'

I may have yelled that last bit.

'Oh,' said John. 'So, um, how did it go?'

'Brilliantly,' I said. 'Like I just said. My friend Jane played your part. And she was better than you.'

'I find that very hard to believe,' said John smugly. And that was it. I knew I didn't want to have anything to do with him anymore.

'John,' I said. 'I think ... we should ...' And I didn't know what to say next. But then I remembered a scene from one of my mother's terrible books in which a heroine breaks up with a selfish boyfriend. And so I said, 'I don't think we should see each other anymore. It's not me, it's you.'

'Wow, Rafferty, don't take everything so seriously,' said John, which was a bit rich coming from him. He couldn't take himself more seriously if he tried.

Anyway, this enraged me even more. 'Oh, I'm sorry,' I said. 'Maybe I shouldn't have said we were seeing each other at all. I forgot we weren't actually "boyfriend" and "girlfriend" because you don't like labels. Well, then you probably won't even notice I'm gone. Goodbye!'

And I hung up.

I felt a bit shaky for a second and like I might burst into tears. But I didn't. I felt the way you do when you get off a rollercoaster – shaky but exhilarated as well. I rang Alice and told her what had happened.

'You have done the right thing,' she said seriously. 'But are you okay?'

I thought for a second.

'I actually am,' I said. 'It's weird; it's like a weight has gone off my shoulders.'

And it really is.

Of course, I am still a bit freaked out. And I am still a bit stressed about the last show. Who knows if we can pull off our triumph for a second time? I am a bit worried Vanessa will let her first night go to her head and start improvising new songs, or something (I wouldn't put it past her, seriously). Today felt like it was going on forever. Which I suppose is why I found myself going in to Rachel and telling her all about John. And how I had basically dumped him. And why.

'Well,' she said, when I'd finished ranting. 'If it's any consolation, I think you did the right thing. I mean, would you be friends with a girl who didn't listen to you and tried to persuade you that the things you liked were rubbish? Even if she was an interesting person?"

'Um, no, of course not,' I said.

'Well, then,' said Rachel. She looked at me. 'Come on, I'll make you my special hot chocolate as a reward.'

Rachel's special hot chocolate is a wondrous thing. She puts cream and cinnamon and God knows what else in there and it tastes delicious. She won't tell anyone the secret of its success and she only makes it for other people on special occasions (the last time she made it for me was when Paperboy went to Canada). Anyway, it is very soothing and I feel a lot better now. Better than I have in ages. Which is good because now I've got to go to school for the very last show. Yikes.

SUNDAY ☼

It's all over. I am very, very tired now because I was up really late last night, and I'm going down to Cass's house to continue our celebrations this afternoon, but I have to document our triumph.

Because we did it again!

I was still nervous when we were all backstage getting our make-up done and changing into our costumes. Ms Byrne and Cathy were walking around saying encouraging things.

'Come on, girls,' said Cathy. 'You can do it one more time. Channel the spirit of *Mary Poppins*!'

But there were a few moments at the start when it kind of seemed like we weren't channelling very much and it wasn't going to go well. Jane stumbled over her words in one scene, which threw Vanessa off her game, and for a few lines it was like seeing arrogant Vanessa herself on stage, not nice, sweet Mary Poppins. But as the scenes went on, it all started to come together (the chorus were excellent as usual, of course).

And Sam was even better than last night. It was like all his fear had gone. Actually, I got chatting to him during the interval – we both went to collect cartons of juice at the same time. I'd never really talked to him before, but it turns out he's actually not that shy and nervous when you talk to him properly.

'Thank God for your friend Jane,' he said. 'I had the fear that I was going to have to do John's stuff. The thought of putting on that bowler hat was giving me nightmares. I even did a comic about it.'

So it turns out the reason Sam was covered in ink is because he does comics. He showed me one on his phone and it was really cool – the pictures were great and the story looked funny. It was about a boy and a girl who are friends and do silly stuff and solve crimes.

'I do them with my friend Lucy who goes to Mary's,' he said. 'She writes and I draw.'

It kind of made me want to do a comic myself. Maybe that could be my next artistic endeavour?

When it was over, lots of us went out to talk to people in the audience. Cass's parents were there, along with her brother Nick and her guest of honour Liz. It was actually really nice to see Liz again. I feel bad about being jealous of her. When me and Cass came out, she ran over and gave Cass a huge hug, and then she hugged me too.

'I can't wait to play with Hey Dollface again!' she said enthusiastically. I was just about to say I couldn't wait for the band to start up again when I saw a terrifying sight over Liz's shoulder.

It was Mrs Harrington. I tried to sneak away while Cass stood in front of me acting as a human shield, but she saw me.

'Rebecca, love!' she cried, beaming at me. Next to her was a surprisingly normal-looking man.

'This is my husband Gerard,' she said. 'We're both very excited about meeting your mammy!'

'Hi, Rebecca!' said Gerard.

'I'm really sorry, Mrs Harrington,' I said, 'but there was a ... a last minute change of plan and she had to go last night instead.'

Mrs Harrington looked really disappointed. So did her husband. I felt more guilty than ever. Which is the only explanation I can think of for what I did next. 'It was a writing emergency,' I said. 'She's ... she's in the middle of a book and she had to meet with her editor. And to apologise to you both, she says she'll name a character in the book after you!'

I don't know what came over me. One minute I am making rules to behave better, the next I am telling insane, barefaced lies to my own teachers!

On the plus side, it did cheer Mrs and Mr Harrington up. They looked very happy as they left. But I don't think that this is a good thing. I have a feeling I will never hear the end of this. Oh dear.

Anyway, I forgot about Mrs Harrington when I went backstage because Ms Byrne and Cathy had a surprise for us.

'To say thank you for all your hard work,' said Cathy, and she smiled and didn't look intimidating or serious at all. They'd ordered a big feast of pizza and fizzy drinks and posh little cakes. It was a surprise after-show party! Someone put music on and people started dancing. Then Vanessa and Karen started singing along, but it was actually quite funny rather than annoying. Especially when Bike Boy and Sam joined in. It was brilliant. Maybe I was in some sort of post-show haze of love for humanity because not even the sight of Karen draped all over Bernard the Fairytale Prince (who had come both nights, he really is devoted) could dampen my mood. We were all really giddy.

'Don't eat too much,' said Ms Byrne. 'I don't want any of you getting sick. Don't forget, it's back to normal life on Monday.'

It didn't feel like normal life until the party was finally over. But then, suddenly, it did. We found ourselves packing up the costumes and throwing pizza boxes and Coke cans into bin bags.

'Everything's going to be pretty dull now, isn't it?' said Ellie sadly, shoving some plastic cups into the bin bag.

'Yeah,' I said, picking up my coat. 'I suppose it will.'

And then my positive mood from the afternoon started to ebb away. I mean, Paperboy was gone forever. Now John was gone too. Not that this is a bad thing. I mean, what sort of boyfriend refuses to hold hands with you in public? AND criticises your mum? It's okay for me to do it, obviously. But not him.

But still, for weeks everything had been exciting. We'd had the show to look forward to. Something new was happening every day. I was all excited about John. And now it was all over. Everything. And it had been so much fun. It had made me cheer up and stick to my rules. I was starting to worry that I would accidentally go back to my old mopey state as Cass, Alice and I walked slowly through the corridor on our way to the car park, where our parents were waiting for us.

'I can't help feeling – and this is totally not a mope, I'm not breaking my rule,' I said. 'But I can't help feeling that there's nothing to look forward to now. I mean, the show is over. We'll be back to our boring old lives on Monday. And then what'll we do?'

And I sighed. I couldn't help it. It had been a very long couple of days. And now everything was starting to feel so flat.

'But,' said Alice, 'my wrist is nearly better.' And she lifted up her cast and waved it about. 'This will be off in a week!'

'And once it is,' said Cass, 'we can finally organise that gig with Bad Monkey. Liz talked to a place in town that will let us do an under-eighteens gig on a Saturday afternoon. We just have to pick a date.'

'Oh,' I said.

'And once we've played one gig, we can play another one,' said Alice. 'Richard says we should all band together, us and Bad Monkey and the Wicked Ways, and put on lots of afternoon shows and, like, get a little music scene going. So we can look forward to that. And then we can try and record something! Richard says he'll show us how to do it. He has all the right software and he says it's quite easy really.'

'And we can write lots of new songs,' said Cass. 'Just think what you'll be able to write about John! You can write about him poncing about in that coat. And having tantrums like a little baby.'

'Ooh, yes,' said Alice.

It's true, I can. And in fairness to John, selfish baby he may be, but since I met him I really have started writing more. Think of all my poems! I bet I'll be able to write better songs than ever now. And I suppose I'll always be grateful to John for encouraging me to write stories again. I'm not going to stop now.

'I suppose,' I said, 'there's quite a lot to look forward to after all.'

'Exactly!' said Cass. 'Lots of stuff. Gigs! And songs! And then it'll be the summer and we can do loads of mad things! And, I dunno. At some stage, you might even meet someone who stays in the same country AND isn't an evil selfish traitor. I mean, we're nearly fifteen! Anything can happen!'

I suppose she's right. In fact, I know she's right. Because if the last few months have taught me anything, it's that even when things seem boring and you feel like nothing good will ever happen again, something cool and fun and interesting and exciting always turns up eventually.

It's like a rule.

THE END

The Real Rebecca

My name is Rebecca Rafferty, and my mother has ruined my life. Again.

I didn't mind her writing boring books for grown-ups. But now she's written one about an awful girl my age and everyone thinks it's me!

Including the boy who delivers our newspapers, aka Paperboy, aka the most gorgeous boy in the whole world. Oh, the shame!

And if that wasn't awful enough, the biggest pain in my class wants to use my 'fame' to get herself on the reality show 'My Big Birthday Bash'.

I've just got to show everyone the REAL Rebecca. But how?